A Deadly Secret

The Deadly Series
Book 2

R.M. Connor

A Deadly
Secret

Book 2

R.M. Connor

By R.M. Connor

The Deadly Series

A Deadly Affair

A Deadly Secret

ISBN-13: 9781736713914

Cover design by: Cover Villain
Editing: Black Quill Editing
Formatting: Champagne Book Design

Printed in the United States of America

A Deadly Secret

A Deadly
Secret

To Dilly & Dally
It doesn't matter how much time you spend dilly-dallying as
long as you keep reaching for the stars.

Chapter 1

Maisie stooped in front of the oven. She opened the door and placed her hand above the top rack. Her long, chestnut-colored hair pulled up into a high ponytail, swept over her shoulder as she shook her head. She closed the door and took a step back to stand next to me.

I crossed my arms and stared at the oven in quiet disdain. The soft ticking of my watch reminding me we were running out of time.

"What are we going to do?" She glanced at me; her brows drawn together.

With a heavy sigh, I untied my apron and tossed it on the small, flour-dusted island in the center of the kitchen. A wave of white powder rushed off to litter the floor as the apron landed. There was one hour until The Witches Brew opened and we had nothing more than wet batter and empty trays.

"I'll call Eugene," I muttered, pushing through the swinging half-doors that separated the kitchen from the café.

It'll be fine, I mocked myself, we still had one oven that worked. What could possibly go wrong?

1

Behind the counter, I picked up the phone and dialed the number to Fletcher's Hardware. I leaned against the wall with one boot propped up behind me. The café was dim. The small fairy lights strung from the ceiling reflected warmly off the black countertop. I stared out of the large window at the front of the café while I waited for the recorded message to finish. The sun was peeking through the trees in ribbons of yellows and blues, rising earlier now that it was mid-December.

The machine on the line beeped, and I pleaded for Eugene and his son, Michael Fletcher, to come as soon as possible. I even offered to make each of them a dozen muffins of their choice once the ovens were fixed. Who could resist a fresh batch of muffins?

Maisie pushed through the swinging doors, carrying two large plastic containers of batter. She laid them on the counter. "I'm going to run home and bake the muffins. Hopefully, I'll be back before we open." She pulled on her olive-colored, fleece-lined jacket. She smoothed a few loose strands of hair away from her face and then picked up the containers and rushed out of the café.

I glanced at my watch. There was no way she'd make it back in time, especially since she had to walk home. Following her to the wrought-iron fence surrounding the patio, I opened the gate for her.

"Hurry back!" I yelled as she power-walked down the street.

Our black cat—save a white crescent-moon-shaped patch of fur above his eyes—stretched on top of one of the black, round tables outside on the patio. The little bell around his neck jingled as he jumped off, sprinting to catch up with

Maisie. The street glittered with early-morning frost and a frigid gust of wind wrapped around me. I pulled the thin, red-and-black flannel shirt tighter around my body and watched until she turned a corner and disappeared.

Walking back into the café, dread washed over me. Soon I would be bombarded with tired and hungry patrons expecting their favorite baked goods, without anything to give them. The door chimed and I spun on my heels toward the sound, instantly kicking myself at my forgetfulness to lock it behind me. My best friend, Tessa Anderson, stepped inside, already stripping her jacket off, and looked at me with a single raised brow.

"I just saw Maisie running down the street." She walked to the counter and slid onto a black stool. Unwrapping the scarf from around her neck, she pushed her thick, wavy black hair from her shoulders and fixed her bangs to lay neatly on her forehead. She spent more time 'fixing' her bangs that I often wondered why she kept them. Her bright green eyes twinkled as a grin graced her lips. "Did the oven finally crap out?"

I grunted a response, leave it to Tessa to rub my nose in it. She'd warned me about the ovens, but being the stubborn person I was, I had brushed it off. Narrowing my eyes at her, I pressed a finger against my mouth, desperately trying to hide my smile before she had a chance to say "I told you so." I grabbed a to-go cup and filled it with coffee. She had been stopping by before we opened every morning for the last three weeks. I glanced at my watch—she was even earlier today. I sat the cup on the counter and wrapped my hands around it.

"*Evigilo,*" I whispered the spell, my fingertips tingled as the magic rushed through them and into the cup. The dark liquid rippled, absorbing the wake-up spell—my secret ingredient in the highly sought-after Hocus Focus coffee.

Tessa had only recently discovered I was a witch, and in return, I had been surprised to learn she was a psychic. She could see the past and the future, but her visions weren't always clear. Sometimes they were grainy images or just a feeling. Sometimes she didn't see or feel anything. She had spent the last two months blaming herself over the death of my most recent employee, Leah Crane. Tessa had sold her a necklace from her antique store, Odds 'n' Ends, that had been possessed by an evil spirit.

She had grown up with her grandmother telling her tales of the Wildewoods and what their magic could do. As well as stories of a curse placed upon them, which happened to be true. From the moment we met, Tessa had suspected I was one of the Wildewood witches.

Our heritage ran deep in Wildewood. Our magic was directly tied to the town, and because of the curse, only within city limits could our magic be used. Having grown up in foster care since infancy, I had just learned what I was.

I pushed the cup toward her and she perked up, her waves bouncing around her shoulders. "I might need you to double that. Odds 'n' Ends is nowhere near ready for the Christmas sale tomorrow."

"I can come by during the break and help," I offered, pouring myself a cup of coffee.

Wildewood usually hosted a Christmas Festival in which all the shops had big blowout sales. Town Square would be lit up, Christmas music playing, and dozens of activities to entertain children. Our 'beloved' Madam Mayor decided to skip it this year, probably having something to do with the murder of her almost son-in-law at the Halloween Festival. But she would still be hosting her annual Christmas party. (Yippee). The shops around town were still trying to get rid of their inventory, but there would not be the large crowds of out-of-towners this year.

I curled my lips, watching as Tessa poured an ungodly amount of sugar into her coffee. "You sure?" She tasted it and then added another spoonful. "I could really use the help."

I handed her the lid to her cup as she scooted off the seat. "I'll be there."

"Thanks, Riley. You're a lifesaver." She put her coat back on and stuffed her scarf into a pocket. "Maybe you'll even find something for Ethan while you're there."

Waving goodbye, I dismissed the thought with a chuckle. Ethan Mitchell and I had been dating for almost two months now. This would be our first Christmas together. Do I make a big deal about it? Would he? Or should I play it cool and act like I'd spent many Christmases with different boyfriends over the course of my life?

This was also going to be my first Christmas with my sister. What if I got us all matching pajamas? I laughed out loud at the image of the three of us and Bean sitting around the living room in matching pajamas Christmas morning as we exchanged presents. The image faded as I remembered Maisie and I still hadn't decorated our tree. Hell, we didn't even have a tree.

This was a Christmas of firsts, and we all seemed to be doing a piss-poor job.

I wanted to do everything I imagined we would've done together as children—gingerbread houses, hanging stockings, decorating the house, and, well, a tree. I wanted us to start making our own traditions, but I hadn't expected those traditions would be doing absolutely nothing. Maybe I was putting too much pressure on it.

I checked my watch again. Twenty-five minutes until the café opened. It was official, Maisie would not be back in time. I grabbed the leftover muffins from the fridge and placed them in the small, glass, domed cake stands on the counter then wiped the tables down one last time.

Spinning in a slow circle, trying to find something else to do, I sighed. We usually spent the hour before The Witches Brew opened baking.

Wait—there *was* something I could do.

I walked into the kitchen and opened the oven door, thinking of one last-ditch effort to make the oven work. Why hadn't I thought of this earlier? I snapped my fingers. "*Accendere.*"

The light above the stove turned on. Okay. That didn't work. I snapped my fingers again and it turned off. I narrowed my eyes, focusing on the heating element.

Take two: I repeated the spell and the element glowed an orange-red.

"Yes!" I shouted into the kitchen.

I said the spell again; the third time would be the charm, right? I did a little happy dance, a wiggle of my bum and my hands waving over my head, and then heard a pop. I stopped dancing. The smell of smoke wafted toward me, a spark glittered in the dark oven, and then it grew into a flame. Shit!

I ran toward the back door and grabbed the fire extinguisher. Spraying the white foam into the oven, it doused the flame until it was nothing more than tendrils of smoke. I lowered the extinguisher to my side and placed a hand over my racing heart. After a few deep breaths, I set the extinguisher on the floor. The oven was a mess, coated in the white film. I should have just left this to the professionals. With even more wreckage than before, I walked back into the café and grabbed the phone. Pressing the redial button, I squeezed the bridge of my nose. "Hey. It's Riley, again. I think I need a whole new oven."

Chapter 2

Weaving through the crowded café, I stumbled over a foot sticking out from under a table. The coffee in my hands sloshed from the cups onto the saucers and dripped down, burning my fingers. I wiped them on a rag slung over my shoulder then ran back behind the counter to grab a full carafe to refill the lost liquid.

The door chimed. Maisie burst into the café with the same containers in her arms, except this time they were filled with muffins. I had never been happier to see her. Though we had only been open for a half-hour, the café was far too busy for one person to handle gracefully. I apologized to the customers in front of me and rushed behind the counter to help load the large display case.

"Are you ready to hire another person now?" Maisie said for the hundredth time since we lost Leah.

I opened my mouth to respond but snapped it shut when Ethan walked through the door. He wore a dark-blue pair of scrubs with a white, long-sleeved thermal shirt underneath that hugged his broad form in all the right places. I stood, wiping my palms on my apron. I could already smell his musky, vanilla scent. His smirk reached his eyes, having caught me staring, and his dimples deepened.

Ethan worked at the animal clinic on the street behind us. His father owned it and wanted him to take his place when he retired. He had moved away from Wildewood to gain a degree in Veterinary Science, but Ethan aspired to be a photographer, which was a big leap from all the schooling under his belt.

He pushed his honey-colored hair behind an ear as he reached the counter. Leaning on his elbows, he pressed his lips to mine. As he pulled away, his baby-blue eyes glimmered. He looked me over, causing my cheeks to heat up.

"Can I get two to-go cups of Hocus Focus?" His lips were close enough to mine I could almost taste them.

Maisie handed me the cups; her attention fixated on Ethan—completely unaware of the moment we were sharing. "Will you please talk to her about hiring another waiter?"

Ethan gave Maisie a playful wink, then turned his attention back to me. His lips were drawn in a thin line, and I could tell he was trying not to smile, but the corners of his mouth twitched, giving him away. "Still arguing about that?"

I filled up the paper cups. "We aren't arguing."

"I'm arguing," Maisie retorted as she moved around the display case. "She's ignoring me."

Ethan looked around the room, returning his gaze to me with a raised eyebrow. "It might not be a bad idea. It's been pretty busy."

I rolled my eyes with a huff, then stuck my tongue out like a proper adult. "I don't need you two ganging up on me."

"I'll see you tonight." He kissed my cheek, picked up his to-go drinks, then exited the café.

Maisie elbowed me. "See? Even Ethan agrees, we need help."

Flicking my eyes to the ceiling, I sighed. "Fine. I'll stop by *The Tribune* and place a help wanted ad."

"No need. We can place one in the window." Maisie clapped her hands in triumph.

I folded my arms over my stomach as I watched her grab an already-made sign from underneath the register that read *Help Wanted*. She'd evidently been planning on me saying yes this whole time.

The phone rang, and with a satisfied look on her face, Maisie answered it. She covered the mouthpiece with her hand and whispered, "It's Eugene. They're coming over."

Handing a muffin across the counter to someone who had been waiting patiently, I mouthed "Thank God." It was bad enough that we were down both ovens for the regular shifts at The Witches Brew, but we were catering coffee and cakes at the Mayor's Christmas party tomorrow night. We could bake at home, but the café was much closer.

The bell chimed and Officer Pete Kelley waddled inside, pulling his pants up by his tactical belt. I waved, smiling. Pete had been my late father's partner on the Wildewood Police Force and had become something of a surrogate uncle to me.

"Morning, girls." He looked into the almost-empty display case and his smile faltered. "Slim pickings this morning, huh?" Pete could never resist a muffin, or anything sweet for that matter.

"Don't worry. I saved your favorite." I grabbed the very last espresso chocolate chip muffin from the back of the case. Maisie poured him a cup of Hocus Focus and placed it in front of him before busying herself at the register.

The door chimed again and Pete's partner, John Russell, walked in. He removed his hat, showing a fresh crewcut, and placed it under his arm as he weaved through the café. John and Pete were polar opposites. Where Pete was friendly and chatty, John had a perpetual frown and didn't say much.

Russell, with his tall, thin frame, sat next to short, round Pete.

"Officer Russell," I gave him a slight nod and a strained smile. "What will you have?" He rarely came into the café, so he didn't have a 'usual.'

"Earl Grey, to go," his tone was less than pleasant. He never drank coffee, that much I knew. I poured hot water into a to-go cup, dropped a teabag in, and placed the lid on to hold the drawstring in place.

"You really should try a muffin." Pete pushed his plate toward John, who looked at it and shook his head, pushing it back.

I crossed my arms, thinking: one day, I'll win you over, John Russell. One day. Hopefully, that day would be soon because Pete was about to retire, and then who would give me juicy details about things going on around town?

"Come on, Pete." Russell patted him on the back. "We don't have time to gossip." Ah, Russell was fully aware of Pete's chatter. I stifled a laugh as both men stood. "Thanks for the tea, Riley."

A few minutes passed and Eugene and Michael Fletcher walked through the door. Built like a bull, Eugene had scars all over his arms and a few on his face, most likely from work-related injuries. His thinning white hair gave away his age, though you'd never notice since the man rarely stopped tinkering with something that needed "fixin'." His son was taller by a few inches, his onyx-colored hair buzzed short. The smell of lumber mixed with grease became stronger as they moved closer to the counter.

Eugene patted me on the shoulder, puffing out his chest. His voice boomed over the chatter filling the café, "Having a rough time with appliances, are ya?"

Pushing out my bottom lip, I responded, "You could say that."

I escorted them through the swinging doors into the kitchen, taking note of both men hesitating at the sight. Michael walked to the pair of ovens, he lowered onto his haunches and touched the white residue from the fire extinguisher. He stood, rubbing the residue between his pointer finger and thumb, and looked at me with a furrowed brow.

I pushed my hair behind my ears, my cheeks blossoming with heat. "Don't ask."

"Let us have a look at the other and see what we can do." Eugene placed his bright-red toolbox on the island then lowered to his knees in front of the open oven door.

"Thanks, guys." I hurried back into the café to help Maisie.

She busied herself at the register, and I made my rounds to each table, filling cups and offering to take empty plates. Setting a few dishes into the sink behind the counter, I heard the two men in the kitchen arguing. I moved closer to the display case and 'inspected' the remaining muffins.

"Dad, you have to drop it," Michael pleaded.

"Someone got to them," Eugene responded. "Something's—"

"Just stop it. Please. You're going to get yourself hurt, or worse," Michael interrupted.

He pushed through the doors and I let out a mousy yelp.

Spinning on my heels toward him, I watched his chest heave as he sucked in a deep breath.

Brows scrunched, and jaw squared, his tongue darted out, wetting his lips. "Hey, Riley. I'm going to run back to the store and see if we have a heating element for your oven in stock, but . . ." he paused, tensing when his father came to stand behind him.

"Your ovens are pretty outdated," Eugene said, wiping his hands on a towel.

"Can it be fixed?"

A smile touched Eugene's eyes. "You know I can fix just about anything."

I handed both men a cup of coffee. "I don't know what I'd do without you two."

"I'll be back." Michael patted the counter then moved through the crowd gracefully. He had his father's muscular build, a little leaner and much taller, but just as light-footed.

I caught Eugene watching his son walk out the door. His lips turned down and his chin quivered. What could be going on between them? Eugene cleared his throat, turning to me, the seriousness on his face replaced with a weak grin that didn't touch his eyes. "I'm gonna get to work. We'll head to Twin Falls later to get you a replacement."

Chapter 3

After the café closed for lunch, I bundled up and sprinted down the street toward Odds 'n' Ends. The musty smell of old things mixed with cinnamon from the bowls of potpourri scattered around the store overwhelmed my senses. The door shut behind me, closing off any and all fresh air. During warmer months, Tessa would prop the door open to help with the smell. But it was around thirty degrees outside and that just wasn't an option right now.

Tessa popped up from behind a bookcase near the back. She had pulled her waves into a messy bun that rested on top of her head. Her bangs were pushed to the side. Deep creases between her eyes softened when she spotted me.

"I'm so glad you're here." She dropped a book on the top of the bookcase and a plume of dust lifted around her. Swatting at it, she sneezed.

I walked to the back of the store, scanning the shelves, and purposely looked away from the row of watchful porcelain dolls. Sitting outside of her office was an old trunk. The same one that had carried the necklace that led to Leah's death. The rest of its contents were still missing. No one knew who or what had emptied it. Madam Mayor had been in a tizzy for weeks, scouring the town for magical items only to come back empty-handed. It wasn't easy to find what you were looking for when you didn't know what it looked like.

A pile of handbags laid next to the trunk. "Do you need help with those?"

Tessa ran a hand over the top of her head. "I'm hoping to get rid of them during the sale." She picked one off the floor. "Who doesn't love a good bag?" She hooked it on a rolling clothing rack.

I pointed to a brown, floppy bag on the top of the pile. "*Surgere.*"

The bag rose into the air, floating slowly as I moved my finger toward the clothing rack. The straps slipped into a small, metal hook.

Tessa grinned and squealed. "If you do that, I'm going to finish my sign." She backed up into the bookcase. It wobbled and I bared my teeth, waiting for it to fall and cause a domino effect through the store. She grabbed it, another cloud of dust rising and with it, a fit of sneezes came from Tessa. Four in a row, I was impressed. "I feel as cluttered as my store today," she mumbled, sneezing again while moving around the bookcase toward the register.

Chuckling under my breath, I lowered to the floor with my legs crossed in front of me and continued to hang the bags with a flick of my wrist. To fill the silence, I called from my spot loud enough for Tessa to hear me, "Have you heard from Samantha?" After the death of her fiancé, Trey Brewer, Samantha had left Wildewood without saying goodbye, even to Tessa, and they had been lifelong friends.

"I talked to her a few days ago. She told me to give you her love," Tessa responded.

I glanced through the aisle to see her leaning over the counter as she worked on her sale sign. Twisting my lips, I decided not to call bull crap. I had a suspicion Samantha blamed Maisie and me for Trey's death. She had very little love for me that much I was sure of.

Wrinkling my nose at a large, black tote that rose upside down, I motioned for it to turn right side up. A small, gray canister fell from one of its pockets, landing with a muted plop on the remaining bags. I leaned over, picked it up, and pulled the black lid off the top.

Pouring a used roll of film into my hand, I couldn't help but think of what it contained. A child's birthday party, or sunny days on vacation. I could get Ethan to develop it. He had recently set up his darkroom in a spare bedroom in his house. Whoever it belonged to, I might be able to find them and return the pictures.

I just hoped it wasn't an X-rated roll of film. That would be awkward.

Standing, I walked to the counter. "Hey, look what I found." I placed the film in front of her.

She picked it up and her body went rigid, her eyes fluttered closed. It was her tell-tale sign: She was receiving a vision.

Seconds later, she blinked. Her dilated pupils were shrinking, and her muscles relaxed. Her gaze moved up to mine, and she handed the film back. "I think this belongs to you."

"Me?" I palmed the film. I couldn't remember the last time I had used a film camera, but I knew for sure I had never owned that particular bag it had been hiding in.

"You should ask Ethan to develop it." She nibbled the side of her bottom lip.

I put the film back into the canister and pressed the lid close. "What did you see?"

Her gaze dropped to the sign she had been writing. Unlike her store, her handwriting was neat. *Memories make the best gifts.* She tapped the chalk, marking on the word *memories*.

"Whose memories?" I prodded.

Tessa looked back at me, her face lighting up. She skittered down the aisle beside her, the metaphorical lightbulb glowing above her head. Standing on her toes, Tessa cradled an old camera in her hand. "Here." She placed it on the counter in front of me. "I know you haven't found Ethan a present. This would be perfect."

I crossed my arms. She was avoiding the question. Whatever she saw, she must not want me to know. It didn't matter; I would find out eventually. I took the camera and started back toward the pile of bags.

"Riley."

I could feel her standing behind me, and I slowly turned to face her.

She gave me a weak smile. "They're your mother's memories."

My breath caught in my throat and I stepped backward. The canister fell to the floor as I reached out to grab a shelf to steady myself. I closed my eyes, hot tears trying to escape. I swallowed with effort. "My mother?" I croaked. "How?"

My mother had been dead for decades, or so we assumed. She hadn't been seen since Maisie and I were born. How was it possible that something of hers had made its way into Tessa's

17

store then into my hands? I wiped the tears from my eyes with the back of my hand.

Tessa laid her hand on my arm. "You look just like her."

My lips parted. She had seen what my mother looked like? I stared at the canister.

"Have Ethan develop it." She gave me a soft smile. "I'm rarely wrong."

Chapter 4

I hadn't recovered from Tessa's vision. Between distracting myself with the clutter in her store, and picking Maisie up from the café, my mind was still reeling with the prospects of what was on the roll of film. Did I want to know? I swallowed the lump in my throat. I hadn't even told Maisie yet.

"Have you seen Bean?" she asked, walking ahead of me up the porch steps.

"Not since this morning." I made sure to check the chairs on the front porch. Sometimes he napped on the cushions.

Bean wasn't an ordinary cat. He was our familiar. Yes, *our* familiar. We shared him, and though it wasn't common for two witches to share the same one, nothing about our witch-hood was common.

Every set of Wildewoods came in twos—female twins, and only one set per generation. As long as both lived, their powers grew immensely. But that came with a price. One of the twins would become corrupt. The power would consume them, and they would slowly go insane. Someone, a long time ago, had

19

tapped into a well of power and brought a curse upon the lineage. There was only one way to break it: the ultimate sacrifice.

I stepped inside the warm house. Hushed voices trailed through the hallway. I pulled on Maisie's jacket before she could walk any further and placed a finger over my lips, hoping to hear the conversation.

Our deceased Aunt Agatha materialized in front of us and I made a little *iiieee* noise. I hated when she did that. She straightened the floppy, patched-up witch hat sitting on her head and crossed her arms over her chest. "There you two are."

Agatha had passed away a few months before our birth. She'd hoped to save us from the curse that had taken hold of our mother, assuming the ultimate sacrifice was her own life. She jumped to her death, but the curse remained.

"Were you talking to someone?" I looked around but didn't see anyone but us three.

"Who would I be talking to, Riley?" She rolled her eyes toward the ceiling. "The dust mites under the couch?"

She was still wearing the same outfit she had died in: A daisy-print shirt and high-waisted blue jeans. Her feet floated above the wooden floor as she rose to sit on the countertop. I wasn't sure if I'd ever get used to a ghost crashing on my couch. She was translucent, though she could pick things up and touch us—she just didn't do either very often.

"Did you find it?" Maisie asked before Agatha could get in another witty remark.

"Not yet." Agatha leaned back on her hands, swinging her legs. She had been searching for our family grimoire but was having a hard time pinning it down.

"I'm sure it'll turn up." Maisie took off her jacket, hanging it in the hallway closet. "Have you seen Bean?"

"Nope." She lifted her nose into the air. Those two had a strange relationship, one that I would never understand. "I'm sure he'll turn up."

I cupped the film in my hand and slipped it out of my pocket. Maisie watched me as I set it on the counter next to Agatha. I was worried about getting her hopes up, but I didn't want to keep this secret to myself any longer.

"What's that?" she asked, grabbing a box of cocoa rice cereal from the pantry.

I popped open the lid and slid it out. "I found it at Tessa's. She said . . ." pausing, I glanced at Agatha. "They're memories from our mother."

Agatha's brows creased. "Impossible."

Maisie set the gallon of milk down and crossed her arms. "Why is it impossible?"

"Your mother—" she stopped, snapping her jaw shut. "Did Tessa say anything else?"

I shook my head and placed the film back in the canister. "No, just that it felt familiar."

Agatha hadn't been too forthcoming about any information pertaining to our mother. She would get misty-eyed, then irritated whenever we asked questions. The only thing we finally got out of her after we found out what we were was a name.

Angela.

The mother who'd separated us and given us away. Her name left a bad taste in my mouth. It conjured too many emotions. I desperately wanted to know her, to know who she was, but at the same time, I felt bitter toward her. Because of her, Maisie and I had grown up alone, without any family.

I shoved the film back into my pocket, as well as the hurt feelings bubbling to the surface. Maybe it was for the best that she wasn't around to answer my questions. I didn't know if I'd ever be able to forgive her.

A knock came at the door. I looked at Maisie, her eyes were wide, then we both looked at Agatha. She raised her arms with a shrug.

"You have to go," I whispered.

"Go where?" she asked, floating to stand on the floor.

I waved my arms. "Anywhere. Just go."

Agatha crossed her arms, her body a little less see-through.

"Now," I hissed, walking to the door. The person behind it knocked again. She didn't budge. Narrowing my eyes at her, I snapped my fingers. "*Recursus*."

Agatha yelped, her body dematerializing into a thin cyclone of black smoke. The witch hat on top of her head fell to the floor, pressing the cyclone down. Maisie bent to pick up the hat and peered inside. "She's not going to be happy about that."

I turned back toward the door to see Ethan standing in the hallway, his mouth hanging open. Shit. He looked at me, snapping his jaw shut, his lips pressed together. "Riley? I heard a scream. What was—" He looked behind me at Maisie. "Who was . . ."

Maisie picked up her bowl of cereal. "I'm gonna go eat this in my room." She mouthed "sorry" and ducked into her room next to the kitchen.

Rubbing the back of my neck, I gradually raised my chin

to look at Ethan. I wasn't ready to have this conversation but it looked like I didn't have a choice.

"I think we need to talk." I reached out to take his hand, fear closing my throat at the thought of him pulling away. His fingers intertwined with mine, and I released the breath I had been holding. I pulled him up the steps to my loft bedroom, loosening my grip on him when I reached the last step.

I paced the length of my room. Ethan leaned against the dresser with his arms crossed over his chest. His gaze followed me from one end to the other. Would he leave? I took a glance at him. The ring of gold in his blue eyes was brighter than usual. Why wasn't he freaking out? Why was he just standing there, watching me? I cleared my throat, stopping a few feet shy of him. "Ethan—"

"What was—I mean . . ." He cleared his throat. "Who was that?"

Agatha. I ran a hand over my face. How did I explain her? Why couldn't she have just *poofed* herself out of sight so I didn't have to deal with this? I straightened my posture. My mouth seemed to be salivating at an unreasonable rate and I swallowed several times to clear it. "That was my . . ." I looked up at him, feeling more scared than ever to tell him my secret. Just get straight to the point, Riley. Rip the band-aid off! "That was my dead aunt." There. That wasn't so hard, was it? But my heart was pounding so loud in my ears I was sure Ethan could hear it.

He raised an eyebrow. "So, a ghost?"

Wait. What? Why wasn't he freaking out? I would be. Nodding, I lowered my eyes to the floor. "Yes." I prepared myself to rip off another band-aid. I took in a deep breath, then said, "Ethan I'm a—"

23

"I know."

His words caught me off guard and I jerked my head up to look at him. A grin formed on his lips. He motioned for me; his hand outstretched. I cocked my head, curiosity flooding me. He knew? How?

"Come here." He grabbed one of my arms, tugging me closer. His hand trailed down to find mine. I was at a loss for words. I had been so scared for him to learn my secret, so afraid it would be too much for him to deal with.

He pressed his lips gently against my temple and my shoulders sagged, my muscles loosening. "I've been spending a lot of time over here," he started, a dimple forming in his right cheek as he smirked. "You two aren't as sneaky as you think." He kissed my jaw, right below my ear, and whispered, "Especially when you're tired."

"Why didn't you ever—" I shook my head, furrowing my brows. "You aren't freaked out?"

"We all have our secrets, Riley." He pulled me closer, our bodies pressed tight. "Especially in this town."

I leaned back slightly, his arms keeping me from taking a step backward. "Yeah? What's your secret?"

Ethan chuckled. "What secret?" His grin widened. "I'm an open book. I have no idea what you're talking about."

I started to protest but his lips found mine and all rational thought faded. Way to change the subject, Mister Mitchell. His large hands roamed my back, trailing down to my rear. He lifted me up and I wrapped my legs around his waist. His secret could wait. I felt so relieved that the one man I had finally decided to take a chance on wasn't scared of me. He wasn't going to run away, even after finding out what I was.

Together, we fell onto the bed, our lips parting only to take a breath. Ethan ran his hand down my side, stopping at my hip. He opened his eyes, looking down as his hand slid into my pants. "What's this?" He pulled the film canister from my pocket.

"An old roll of film." I tangled my fingers in his hair, pulling him back to me.

"What's on it?"

I let out a sigh and removed my hands from around him to prop up on my elbows. He sat on his knees, my legs loosening their hold around his waist. He popped the lid off. The roll of film looked tiny in his hand.

"I have no idea. Can you develop it for me?" Without waiting for an answer, I took it and tossed it on the other side of the bed. The film could wait. I, however, could not.

The bathroom door shut and I froze. Ethan's lips trailed down my neck. "Hold on." I raised my hand in the air, toward the opening of the loft. *"Auribus tantum."*

"What was that?"

He couldn't see it, but there was a sheen of magic at the opening of the stairs, blocking all sound from going through. My own version of a soundproof room. Placing my hands on his upper arms, I pulled him back down. "No one can hear us now."

Ethan's grin grew more mischievous. He growled as he buried his face in my neck, the scratchy shadow of his beard causing a giggle to burst from my throat.

Chapter 5

The following evening, I arrived early to Town Hall, having volunteered to set up the buffet table for the mayor's Christmas party, and was almost done layering cupcakes on white, tiered stands. Maisie would be coming shortly to bring hot coffee. Mike, from Mike's, Wildewood's only bar, had dropped off appetizers. The mayor and he didn't get along, so it was surprising he had offered, though he still refused the obligatory invitation to come to the party.

Butterflies filled my stomach. I had never been a 'prominent figure' anywhere in my life. I had a tendency to keep my head down, but that no longer seemed an option here. Picking up a cupcake, I caught a glimpse of movement out of the corner of my eye. The hair on the back of my neck stood as I turned to look. Putting down the cupcake, I wiped my hands on my apron and followed it toward the front door. I saw another shadowy movement and turned, facing the stairs that led down to Esther's vault. It was a room of secrets. A place she stored magical items known to cause problems.

Madam Mayor was a Keeper, another line of witches with roots deeply tied to Wildewood.

She protected the inhabitants of the town, which to me, meant the residents were all some type of supernatural being. Esther had caught me trying to use a spell on her daughter, Samantha, after her fiancé had been murdered. If not for that incident, I was positive I would never have found out Esther was a witch.

I heard the vault door creak open and walked toward the steps. A sliver of light poured out into the dark landing. There it was, unlocked. Looking around, I didn't see any more shadows. I gripped the railing, my steps slow and soft, then I made my way down to the room. Just close the door, I told myself. I have no business being here. As my hand touched the door to push it closed, I jumped at the sound of a book falling off the shelf in the very back.

"Just leave it." I bit my bottom lip and turned to look behind me. I was still alone at Town Hall; Esther hadn't returned from doing whatever mayor-y thing she was busy with. No one would know. What could it hurt to see what had fallen?

I walked into the room but my steps faltered. No. I couldn't do it. This was a secret room of the mayor's. I shouldn't be in here. I turned around and began to walk back up the steps when I heard another thud. Ever so slowly, I turned to see a very thick, very large book wrapped in brown paper at my feet.

Well, since it wasn't in the room anymore . . . I bent to pick it up and opened the front cover. Sucking in a breath, I shook my head. It couldn't be . . . but it was. *The Wildewood Grimoire.*

The mayor had it the whole time.

The door to the vault slammed shut. The book fell to the

ground as I jumped. I scooped it off the floor and as I scrambled up the steps, I shoved the book into my bag hanging by the front door. I took a deep breath to calm my racing heart. Who the hell had done that?

I hurried into the bathroom and splashed cold water on my face. My fingers gripped the sides of the sink as I stared at my reflection. Paler than usual, pupils dilated. I reached for a folded paper towel, almost knocking over a small flower arrangement of purple, red, and white flowers. Grabbing the short, round vase before it could topple over, I settled it back in place. I pressed the scratchy paper towel to my face and took a deep breath.

I left the bathroom to finish setting out the cupcakes. Placing the last snowflake cupcake—white buttercream with tiny iridescent flakes—on the top tier, someone grabbed me from behind, wrapping their hands around my waist. I screamed, turning on my heels, ready to smack Mister Handsy. My hand fell short as my eyes took in Ethan smiling back at me.

"Good grief." I took in a deep breath and laughed nervously. "You scared the shit out of me."

He pressed his lips against mine, clearly unconcerned over the heart palpitations he had caused. "I thought I'd come by early to help you." He glanced behind me at the three five-tier stands filled with cupcakes. "But it seems you don't need any help."

"I work pretty fast when I'm not distracted." I poked him in the chest.

He pulled me closer, peering down at me, and playfully bit my bottom lip. "I like being your distraction."

I glanced over at the hallway where my bag hung. I had enough distractions right now as it stood. His lips found mine again, and I melted into his warm body. Ethan was always warm, even when it was freezing outside. I found myself wanting more, deepening our kiss, and didn't hear the door open. Someone cleared their throat behind Ethan and my eyes popped open.

My cheeks heated when I saw Esther Miller standing behind us, her arms crossed, completely unamused by the show we were putting on. I pulled away, running my fingers over my lips.

"Ethan, would you mind running to The Stop and Shop for a bag of ice?" She wasn't asking.

Ethan sighed as he planted a kiss on my forehead.

"You could ask nicely," I mumbled.

Ignoring me, Esther walked into her office, her heels loud in the quiet building. I stayed next to the buffet table, not sure what to do with my hands, I held them behind my back and tangled my fingers together. I could hear her moving around. Turning my head, I caught another glimpse of the shadow. What the hell was that? Could I now see dead people? I gave myself a mental eye roll. I had a dead person living in my house, of course I could. This wasn't just a regular ghost, if it was one at all. It didn't want me to know who or what it was. It did, however, want me to find the grimoire.

Esther walked out of her office at the same time a thud came from near the front door. I watched as her gaze lowered to the floor. She looked at me and I knew what had just happened. My face flushed, my pulse speeding up. She moved out of view, coming back a second later with the book in her hands.

"Where did you find this?" Her stare was drilling holes into me.

"Um . . . I . . ." I shifted my weight back and forth on my feet.

"How did you get into my vault?" She took a step closer.

I backed up, hitting the table. "It was open." Finally, I could form words. My heart felt like it was going to beat right out of my chest. There was no joy in being on Esther's bad side.

"You shouldn't have this." She strode toward her office.

I stared at her, dumbfounded, for a few seconds before snapping my jaw shut. Wait—I shouldn't have it? It belonged to the Wildewoods! And I was a Wildewood. I rushed after her. "No, that doesn't belong to you."

The mayor stopped walking, her back still facing me. Her shoulders rose and fell as she took in a deep breath. Slowly turning to look at me, Esther handed it back. "Be careful."

The front door opened and a crowd of people began to pour in. I took a quick glance behind me, then turned back to Esther. Why did I need to be careful? She put a smile on her face then pushed past me to greet the rest of her guests.

Chapter 6

Facing the crowd flowing into the building, I held the book behind my back. My fingers cramped under its weight. I needed to get it back to my bag, but there were too many people standing in the hallway.

Esther greeted Sheriff Manuel Vargas and his wife, Sasha. I had only ever seen him in his uniform, but tonight he wore a black suit with a red tie. His wife hooked her arm, which was wrapped inside a light-gray, faux-fur-cropped jacket, around his. Tall, even without her six-inch heels, Sasha—supermodel thin and a bottle blonde—had a large smile just as shiny as the diamonds she wore around her neck.

I caught a glimpse of Maisie slinking around the crowd with two tall coffee thermoses in her hands. Her cheeks were rosy from the cold, December night air. She sat them on the buffet table beside a stack of Styrofoam cups. "Why are you standing like that?"

"I think we're at the wrong party," I mumbled, taking note of how I was dressed compared to everyone else. Black boots with too many scuffs on the toes, black jeggings with the knees slightly worn, and my over-sized, hunter-green sweater. I must've missed Esther's memo about it being a semi-formal gathering. Where was my fairy godmother when I needed one? Maybe she could *bippity-bobbity-boop* my outfit.

Maisie nudged me with an elbow. The book slid from my grip, landing with a loud *thunk* on the ground. She bent to pick it up. "My, what a big book you have." She flipped to the first page, her mouth opening slightly. She looked at me and asked, "Where did you find this?"

I kept my eyes on Esther. "I'll explain later. Go hide it in my bag."

Maisie looked down at the book. I cleared my throat, getting her attention and cocked my head to the side, mouthing "go." Maisie jerked her head up as Esther strolled toward the table. She pressed her lips firmly together and moved away before Esther could reach us.

"Riley." Esther stood, shoulder to shoulder with me, her back turned toward the other guest. "Please take the apron off. You aren't the help tonight."

My cheeks flushed and I tried to untie the knot in the back, but my fingers fumbled, making it worse. She clicked her tongue, whispering something under her breath, and the apron fell to the floor.

"Thanks." I scrambled to hide it under the buffet table, toeing one of the strings that peeked out from under the red table cloth.

"Try to enjoy the party, Riley." Esther nosed the air and turned back toward the rest of her guests.

Town Hall was not a huge building, and though it wasn't small by any means, it felt as if the whole town had been invited.

The temperature rose from the number of bodies filling the space. Turning away from the crowd, I leaned my nose toward my shoulder, trying to remember if I'd put on deodorant. I was already starting to sweat, though it was probably my nerves more than anything.

I looked around in hopes of finding a corner to stand in, a place out of the way when my eyes locked on Ethan. Relief washed over me. He smiled and hoisted a large bag of ice on his shoulder. The dark-gray sweater he wore lifted to expose a sliver of skin at his waist, and it took all of my willpower not to stare.

A woman walked in front of him, blocking my view for a second. When my eyes refocused, I realized it was Jessica Freki, owner of Lunas Boutique. Her light-brown curls were tamed by a clip at the base of her neck. She gave a quick wave before heading toward a short hallway where the bathrooms were located. I waved back, then realized she was looking past me at her associate, Sophia King. I dropped my hand, hoping no one noticed.

Ethan walked behind me to pour the ice into a large pitcher. He set the remaining ice into a cooler under the table. Sliding his hand into mine, he kissed me on the cheek. His hands were surprisingly warm for having just had ice on them.

I spotted Tessa and relaxed further. All of my people were finally here. She grinned at me and pointed to a small bar set up on the opposite wall outside Esther's office. She curled her fingers as if she were holding a cup, brought it to her lips, then threw her head back. I tugged on Ethan's hand, taking a step toward the bar, but Manuel and his wife blocked my way. Wrinkling my nose, a powerful smell wafted—no—invaded my senses. Patchouli and something else I couldn't quite put my finger on. I breathed through my mouth, but then I tasted it.

I glanced over at the bar, wishing I had something to wash the taste out of my mouth. Ethan unwrapped his fingers from mine, placed another kiss on my cheek, then walked to the bar. He either read my mind or also needed to escape the overpowering smell of Sasha's perfume.

"Riley." Sheriff Vargas nodded at me.

Putting my best fake smile on, I waved, trying to breathe as little as possible. "Sheriff. I'm glad you two made it."

Sasha poked her head from around his shoulder. "Riley Jones?"

I tried to keep the confusion off my face. Did my name mean something to her? We had never been properly introduced. "Yes." I extended my hand out to her. "I own—"

She slapped her husband on the arm. "The Witches Brew! Jessica brings me coffee from your café all the time. I can barely get through my morning without some of your Hocus Focus. I'm dying to know what the secret ingredient is."

A nervous chuckle bubbled up my throat, and I somewhat jokingly said, "I'll be taking that with me to the grave."

Her shiny smile faded. I had a feeling Sasha wasn't used to not getting her way. She moved past my cupcakes, her nose turned up slightly, and grabbed a few chocolate-covered strawberries to set on her plate. Little did she know, I had made those too.

Ethan held a slender glass of shimmering, pale-gold liquid in front of me. I wrapped my fingers around the stem and drank it in one, painful gulp. The champagne hit my stomach and a wave of heat radiated through me, my body tingling. I blinked, trying to focus on the knitted pattern of Ethan's sweater in hopes of deterring the fuzzy feeling growing in my head.

Ethan cocked his head, an eyebrow raised. "You know that wasn't a shot, right?"

Were there shots?

I looked at the bar. Instead of seeing shots as I'd hoped, I saw Jessica Freki heading this way. Her golden-brown eyes narrowed as she looked between Vargas and his wife. I was pretty sure she and Sasha were friends, but that was *not* a friendly look. She stopped in front of them, raising her chin to make eye contact. Jessica was a bit taller than me, putting her at an average height, but anyone standing next to Sasha in her stilettos would seem short.

Hooking my arm in Ethan's, I pulled us toward the bar and away from a rather scorned-looking Jessica. Maisie appeared beside me, the book safe in my bag. She glanced at me; her brows scrunched.

"You okay?"

Leaning over the bar, I picked up another champagne flute. I drank it quickly then nodded as I set the empty on the counter. "Couldn't be better."

"I think she's nervous," Ethan whispered to Maisie.

"Why?" Tessa looked at me. I pursed my lips in response. Her face softened and she placed her hand on mine as I reached for another flute. I pulled my hand away, but her eyes had already dilated, stealing a vision from me. Okay—we needed some 'my best friend is a psychic' rules. "You belong here just as much as anyone," Tessa spoke softly. "Here." She reached into an inner pocket of her jacket and then handed me a small flask. Without care, I took a sip, the contents burning my throat on the way down.

I heard a raised voice behind me. The conversations around

the room quieted, but the Christmas music prevented me from understanding what Jessica was whisper-screaming at Sasha. She had her hands on her hips, her lips thin lines as they pulled away from her teeth. Sasha ran past us, shielding her face with a slender hand.

Jessica crossed her arms and turned her attention to Vargas, who finished his champagne then rolled his shoulders back in a shrug. Jessica threw her hands in the air and stomped away from him. The volume of chatter rose again. My head was starting to spin and I grabbed onto the bar, closing my eyes tight.

I needed water. I blinked my eyes open, waiting for them to focus before making the trek to the bathroom.

"What's going on?" Maisie asked, her attention focused across the room, not on her dear ol' sister.

Eugene and Michael Fletcher walked toward the buffet table. Vargas became noticeably tense, the muscles in his neck tightening. If he tensed much more, his tie might strangle him. Michael looked toward his father and though I could see his lips move as he squeezed his father's shoulder, I couldn't hear a word he said. He walked away from the two men. My smile was greeted with a nod and he continued past us. My gaze followed him until he pushed open the men's bathroom door.

"They're in business together and it's not going well," Ethan answered.

I leaned against Ethan, taking note of his incredibly muscular arm. He glanced down at me and his eyes creased in amusement. I froze, realizing I had been rubbing his bicep, and shoved my hands in my pockets, returning my attention to the other two men.

Eugene moved toward Vargas, his posture stiff. I had never

seen this side of Eugene. He was a happy man, a smile always on his face—except for recently. Vargas squared his shoulders, his chest puffing out.

"Shit," Ethan whispered. He pushed away from the bar, walking toward them.

Maisie handed me another champagne flute, I scowled at it. She tossed hers back and I shrugged, following suit. It looked like we were both feeling a little out of place tonight.

"No more for you." Tessa took the empty flute from my hand.

She was probably right. I was teetering on tipsy, one more drink and I'd probably fall well over the line. Already overheated in my thick sweater, I was tempted to pull it off, but I don't think that's the type of party Esther had in mind.

A woman with wiry, brown waves wedged herself between Tessa and me, forcing me to scoot over, bumping into Maisie. She was a little taller than me, but I think that might have something to do with the thick wedge heels she wore. "Excuse me," she mumbled under her breath, leaning over the bar for one of the few remaining glasses of champagne.

Sorry, I thought, feeling a smile creep on my lips which I hid with a finger pressed against them.

"Natalie Remington." She held her empty hand out to me.

She had a firm handshake. "Riley Jones."

Pulling a few business cards out of her purse, she passed them around. "I just joined Wildewood Realty."

I slipped the card into my pocket. I had no interest in selling either of my properties but she didn't need to know that. I heard a shout and looked over my shoulder. Vargas's face had reddened, his shoulders moving up and down with his heavy breathing. His nostrils flared. Michael stood close to his father, whose hands flexed into fists.

What the hell was going on?

Before Eugene had a chance to respond, Ethan touched his shoulder. Eugene jerked his head to look at him, anger flashing across his face. They exchanged a look, but I couldn't hear what was being said. Eugene's lips moved in response. Ethan put his hand under Eugene's arm, pulling him away.

Then I heard Ethan's voice as the Christmas jingle ended, "It's not worth it. Not here."

Ethan's brows were pinched tight together as he walked with the Fletchers toward the door. Where was Esther? Shouldn't she be dealing with this? I stood on my toes, looking around for her. She was walking through the crowd toward Vargas, her finger pointed at his chest. His head lowered like a dog being scolded by its owner.

"I'll be right back," I whispered, and slipped away to follow Ethan.

The night air instantly cooled me as I stepped onto the porch and pressed my back against the bricks. Ethan and the Fletchers were standing on the sidewalk. Something moved in my peripheral and I turned my head to spot the small shadow—the same one from before. It moved away from the light of the porch.

Ethan shook Eugene's hand. He patted the older man on the shoulder then walked back up the steps.

"Come on." Ethan reached for my hand and led me back inside to Maisie and Tessa.

I looked over the bar at the empty flutes in front of me. What drink was I on? Four? I'd had three earlier . . . I thought

I was saved when the champagne ran out, then Esther had one of her staff members pour another two dozen.

Excusing myself, I walked toward the bathroom, my hand running along the wall just in case my legs got the wobbles. Well, this sucked. I was drunk. My head was swimming and my body was warm—a little too warm. I pushed the bathroom door open and noticed the vase on the counter was on the floor near a stall.

The smell of patchouli clung to the warm air of the bathroom. Rubbing my eyes, trying to keep them in focus, I picked up the vase and saw Sasha's six-inch heels under the stall door. "Hello?" A sharp edge of the vase poked my finger and blood swelled to the surface. Sucking my finger, I looked at the ground. Flowers from the vase were scattered all over the floor. The white tile was slick with water. I set the vase back on the counter, careful to not cut myself again. "Sasha?" I knocked softly on the door. "Are you okay?"

The door gave under my hand and I sucked in a sharp breath. My feet tried to slip out from underneath me as I stumbled backward. I grabbed onto the counter, unable to take my eyes off Sasha. She sat haphazardly on the toilet, slumped over, her head resting against the side of the stall, arms hanging lifeless beside her, fingertips touching the floor. Her mouth hung open, eyes staring sightlessly at the ceiling.

Tessa walked into the bathroom. She looked at me, the floor, and then walked to stand in front of the stall. She gasped, grabbed my arm, and pulled me out of the bathroom.

"Someone call nine-one-one!" she yelled as she pulled me back toward Ethan and Maisie.

The contents of my stomach threatened to come up. I looked back at the bathroom as Vargas ran toward it, he was, after all, an officer. He stumbled out a moment later. His face was pale as he leaned against the wall, his head resting on his arm. I watched his chest rise and fall. He straightened his jacket, his tie, then walked into the middle of the room.

"No one leaves. My wife has been murdered." He pulled his cell phone out and called the station, requesting every available officer to come from next door.

The cheery Christmas music was still playing: "It's beginning to look a lot like Christmas . . ." I slid to the ground against the bar, pulling my knees to my chin. My head was swimming and I was certain if I moved, I'd throw up.

Vargas kneeled in front of me. "Riley, did you see anyone leave the bathroom?"

I shook my head very slow but the movement still sent a wave of nausea through me. Maisie pushed a small circular trash can beside my legs. I grabbed it, placed it on my lap, and wrapped my arms around it. Deep breaths, I reminded myself and tilted my head back to look around the room.

Manuel moved to talk to one of the officers in uniform who had just arrived. Sophia King stood beside him. He patted her back as she covered her face with her hands, and even from this distance, I could make out her sobs.

I tugged on Tessa's pants, and she leaned down. "Who is Sophia to the Vargas'?"

Tessa took a moment to look at the woman, then whispered, "She's their niece."

Chapter 7

I leaned back in my office chair with a cold towel draped over my eyes. The chatter from the café was not helping the pounding in my head. I barely remembered Ethan and Maisie tucking me into bed after the police let us leave. Images of Sasha's lifeless body had filled my dreams all night. Her eyes staring up at the ceiling, the flowers scattered around the floor. I couldn't help but feel guilty. If I hadn't been so focused on my own discomfort, maybe I would've seen something. I wanted to help Vargas find his wife's killer, but I hadn't noticed anyone going into the restroom after Sasha.

I felt terrible for the sheriff. One moment Sasha had been upset with her husband, the next she was dead.

What a tragedy, really.

I was starting to believe any and all Wildewood get-togethers were cursed and that I should seriously consider not attending another one. An unsettling thought hit me: There hadn't been any murders I knew of at any of the town parties or festivals until I moved to town.

If that wasn't a self-esteem killer, I didn't know what was.

Walking out of the office, my stomach felt queasy and my head throbbed under the bright lights. The volume level of the chatter jumped louder the moment I left the hallway. Or maybe that was just me. I rubbed my temple in a slow circular motion, hoping to dull the pain.

Maisie waved me over. She stood on the other side of the counter beside a tall man I had never seen before. I moved toward the coffee machine, wishing I had a way to enchant it and cure my hangover. I could probably figure it out, but I wasn't sure I had the needed mental capacity at the moment.

Maisie cleared her throat. I stopped mid-pour and looked over at her. "This is Zachary Osbourne."

I gave him a little wave.

Maisie narrowed her eyes at me and bared her teeth as she said, "He's here to fill the open position."

My face went slack. I didn't understand a word she said.

"For the extra set of hands we need," she elaborated.

The carafe dropped to the counter and I stuck out my hand to shake his. Not a very good first impression of his potential boss. I looked up to meet his gaze, trying to smile but the light above him was creating a bright halo around his head, sending a painful ping through my own.

I tried not to squint as I looked him over. He had soft features, except for the slight crook of his nose. His eyes were dark brown with specks of gold dancing in his irises. His black hair curled around the crown of his head.

Maisie handed me his application. I glanced at it. The tiny words blurred and my stomach started to turn. I laid the page down and blinked to focus my eyes. "Have you ever worked in hospitality before?"

I placed the cup on the counter. It tilted and sloshed, coffee spilled over the side. I needed to go home and sleep off this hangover.

"No. But"—he stole a napkin and wiped the spilled coffee—"I have experience in taking care of people. I'm a fast learner."

I glanced at Maisie standing behind him. She mouthed "please" with her palms pressed together as if praying. Looking back at Zach, I nodded. "Okay. Want to come back tomorrow evening, say an hour before we reopen?"

He smiled. His incisors were a little pointier than most peoples'. He reached his hand back out to shake mine. "I'll be here."

"Let me get you a menu to study."

Maisie was all but bursting at the seams with excitement. She must have assumed I would say yes to anyone who applied and pulled a menu with a cheat-sheet paper clipped to it from underneath the register.

Zach took it from her. He ducked to miss the door frame as he left. Well, we definitely wouldn't lose him in a crowd.

Maisie crossed her arms, watching him walk past the window. Her lips twitched into a half-smile. "He's pretty cute."

Laughing at her reaction, I retorted, "As long as he can make a decent cup of coffee."

I walked into the kitchen to find a cold bottle of water, deciding coffee was not going to help me, as much as it pained me to say. The cool air in the refrigerator felt like heaven against my face. Closing my eyes, I leaned in further. The nausea subsided a bit.

The swinging doors to the kitchen banged against the wall, and I jumped, barely missing hitting my head on the refrigerator.

A large oven was being wheeled in with Michael guiding it to the empty spot next to the one Eugene had been able to fix.

"Sorry! I didn't mean to scare you," Michael apologized as he removed the straps from around the oven.

A memory came crashing into my already-pained head. Michael had gone down the hallway only minutes after Sasha had stormed off.

He turned to look at me, an eyebrow raised. "Riley, are you okay?" He took a step toward me.

I backed into the refrigerator door. "Yes. Yeah—" I held up the water bottle. "I just needed some water."

He returned to the oven. "Okay. You just look like you've seen a ghost."

A ghost? No. I crept out of the kitchen and back behind the counter. A murderer, perhaps, but not a ghost. Tightening my apron around my waist, I glanced back at the kitchen. He couldn't have been the only person to go into the bathrooms between Sasha storming off and me finding her. Just because I didn't see it, doesn't mean it didn't happen, right? My chest felt tight, and I wanted him to hurry and finish installing the oven.

Filling a cup of Hocus Focus for Maisie, I handed it to her across the counter.

"I think he's going to be a perfect fit," she commented.

I gave her a confused look.

She cocked her head to the side and sighed. "Zach. I think he's going to do well here."

"Oh, right. Sorry, I'm feeling a little off."

"That's understandable." She gave me a weak smile before delivering the coffee to a customer.

My mind was a hundred miles away, or rather, inside the

bathroom of Town Hall. Who would be so brash to kill Sasha in a room full of people? Untying my apron, I placed it near the coffee maker. I strolled over to her in the far-left corner of the café as she was picking up a pile of empty dishes.

"I need to get some air. I'll be back."

The café wasn't too busy, she would be fine for a little while on her own and surely Michael, now a suspect in my book, had no qualms with us.

Chapter 8

The crisp December air dulled the pulsing in my head. I stood outside the fence surrounding the café patio, wishing I had grabbed my jacket as a gust of wind swept down the lane. I looked toward the square. Large, red-and-white striped candy canes bordered the walkway. Christmas lights were strung on the branches of the large oak tree in the middle of the lawn. I heard a loud voice and glanced down the street.

Sheriff Vargas stood outside the hardware store with Eugene. And from the looks of it, he wasn't sheriff today. His white button-down shirt hung half-tucked from his belt line. The fabric was wrinkled as if he had slept in it. The dress shoes on his feet told me he hadn't gone home after the Christmas party.

Their noses almost touched. Vargas poked Eugene's chest repeatedly. Gritting my teeth, I waited for Eugene to turn into an actual bull, but his face remained calm. The words flowing from Vargas' lips were loose and slurred. Eugene's were direct and short. Shoppers and shopkeepers alike were turning their attention to the two men.

My feet moved before my thoughts, and I was walking toward them to try to . . . stop the public scene, I guess, before it got more out of hand. I wasn't sure what was going on, possibly a continuation of their argument the night before. But good grief, weren't there bigger problems now than whatever business they were involved in? And did they really want the entire town to know?

"I wouldn't," a familiar, demanding voice stopped me in my tracks.

The echoed clopping of hurried footsteps made me turn. Esther crossed the street, holding cupcake towers in both hands. She had on a black blazer with ankle-cut black pants. Her gray curls were pulled away from her face, exposing small diamond earrings.

"But they're—" I lowered my voice as she neared. "People are staring."

"Let them. Our dear sheriff is making a fool of himself." She handed me the towers then wiped her hands together. "Such a pity." She placed a gentle hand on my shoulder and turned me away. "The problems those two have are not our concern."

"But it's your town—"

"I'm in dire need of some caffeine. It was a long night," she interrupted then walked ahead of me.

A patrol car passed us. The brake lights flashed as it pulled over to the curb beside them.

Glancing over my shoulder as I hurried after Esther, I saw John Russell stepping out of the car. Eugene moved away, going back inside his store. The two officers stood beside the car until Russell opened the passenger door but it didn't seem Vargas had any interest in leaving just yet.

I caught up with Esther. She took her white handkerchief from the small purse that hung by her side and wiped the seat of one of the black chairs on the patio. "Please be a dear and get me a cup of coffee."

I nodded, finding it strange she was sitting outside, but I had a feeling she was more interested in the argument down the street than she was letting on. I returned quickly with two cups and set one in front of her. I placed a cream-and-sugar set in the middle of the table.

Taking a seat across from her, I glanced down the street. She cleared her throat, bringing my attention back to her. Staring at me, she prepared her coffee. I wanted to watch the scene unfolding in front of Eugene's store, instead of sitting in awkward silence with Esther, but my mind began to wander back to her vault.

"Is there something you would like to ask me?" She stirred her coffee.

As a matter of fact, there was. Esther rarely answered any of my questions, something she and Agatha had in common, so I was not going to pass on the invitation.

"Your vault . . ." I chewed on the inside of my cheek. "It's impenetrable."

"Riley, just ask your question." She sipped the steaming liquid.

"Why was it open?"

Esther shrugged. She brought the cup back to her mouth, her pinkie extended. "Must've slipped my mind."

Narrowing my eyes, I crossed my arms on the table and leaned closer. "Nothing slips your mind."

She flicked her eyes up and set her cup down.

I leaned back against the chair, crossing my arms over my chest. "I think you left it open on purpose."

"Don't be silly. That would be dangerous. You know as well as I do what I store in that room." She gathered up her purse and pushed her chair back to stand.

I heard a car door close, so I looked down the street just in time to see the backlights of the patrol car light up before it pulled away from the curb. I guess John Russell won the argument. I turned back to Esther. "Thank you . . . for forgetting to close the door."

She harrumphed and walked off the patio, leaving her coffee on the table.

The door to the café opened. Michael pushed the empty hand trunk in front of him through the threshold then set it down gently beside my table. "I gave the warranty paper and receipt to Maisie." He propped his arm on the handles.

"Thank you." My nerves were starting to spike again.

"I heard you were the one to find Sasha's body."

I lifted my chin, eyes squinted from the blinding sun.

"Anyone would be feeling a bit off after that, so I'm not going to take your distance personally." The side of his mouth twitched into a sympathetic smile. "I hope they figure out what happened to her before—" He pushed the hand truck back on its wheels.

As he passed me, I stood. "Before what?"

Michael shrugged. "Before our sheriff does something that can't be undone." He walked off the patio.

I stood there with my mouth agape and watched Michael walk down the street back to the hardware store. Wrapping my arms around myself, I watched him until he entered the building. Was the sheriff involved in something that had led to his wife's murder? I didn't know anything about Manuel Vargas, except that he had been the county sheriff for a very long time.

Chapter 9

The rest of the day flew by with my hangover randomly reminding me of its existence—a bout of nausea here, a flash of pain there. I didn't know what Tessa had put in her flask, but whatever it was, I would turn it down at the next party. Though at this point, I might just vow to never attend another party in Wildewood. The register dinged as the last customer paid, he grabbed his to-go box and coffee. Maisie brushed past me into the kitchen. The cold air flooded inside when the door opened. Tessa stepped to the side to let him pass, then dragged herself to the counter.

She sat on one of the stools, twisting to one side then the other as her back popped. I placed the last bit of coffee in front of her with a blueberry scone. She pulled her hair out of its high ponytail then removed the bobby pins that held back her bangs. Fluffing her hair out with her fingers she took a deep breath.

"Long day?" I grabbed a damp rag to start wiping tables.

"Crazy long." She brought the cup of coffee to her nose and breathed in the bitter aroma. Setting it back on the counter, she poured sugar into it.

"That's just normal coffee, by the way." We reserved Hocus Focus for mornings only.

Tessa swiveled the stool to face me. "Good. I plan on going home and crashing. As much as the Christmas season is good for Odds 'n' Ends, it is not good for my aging body or my sanity."

I chuckled. She was only twenty-nine, but I understood the backaches after a grueling shift at the café. "It's almost over." I flicked some crumbs to the ground with the rag. "Hey, how come I didn't know Sophia was the sheriff's niece?" They didn't favor each other, though I had only met Sophia once or twice when I'd gone into Luna's.

"She's his sister's daughter—different last names." Tessa bit into her scone, crumbs falling around her. She mouthed a sorry and turned to eat over the small, white plate. At least I hadn't swept yet.

"I didn't know he had a sister." Actually, I didn't know anything about the Vargas'. "Were she and Sasha close?"

"I don't think so." She stopped talking and I heard a slurp. "The sheriff does a good job of keeping his family life private. I'm not surprised you didn't know who she was."

I remembered how upset Sophia had been when the officer had spoken to her and Vargas. I suppose even if they hadn't been close, losing a family member would still bring the type of pain she had expressed. I didn't even know Sasha and I had been— still was—upset. I felt guilty for not having seen something that could help him find his wife's murderer.

"I'm sure the sheriff has every officer on the case. He'll get to the bottom of it, don't worry." Tessa jumped from the stool then walked around the counter to grab a to-go cup. "Do you guys want a ride home? I don't mind waiting."

Her drooping eyes told a different story. She was tired. I gave her a weak smile. Maisie and I had more to do than I was willing to have her wait on. "Go home. Go to bed. I'll see you tomorrow."

Tessa wrapped her arms around my shoulders and squeezed tight. I locked the door behind her, staring out the glass to the snow-dusted street. I didn't remember anything helpful, but I could do something to express my condolences. I would pick up a sympathy arrangement from Connie Fields, our local florist. I grimaced as the image of the broken vase and scattered flowers over the bathroom floor popped into my mind.

On second thought, maybe I should skip the flowers.

Turning the *open* sign to *closed*. I shook the images of Sasha's lifeless body from my mind as I swept a pile of crumbs into a dustpan. I wondered who could be so bold to murder her in the middle of a crowded party. No one heard anything—no noises of distress. She had to have known her killer, though other than the broken vase, I hadn't seen any signs of a struggle. She could've knocked it over herself. Afterall, she had been pretty upset.

A knot formed in my stomach. Glancing out of the large window at the front of the café, I looked across Town Square to the police station. Now that I was thinking about it, besides the vase, there had been no other signs of foul play. She hadn't been bleeding, hell, there hadn't been any blood on the vase. So, why then did the sheriff immediately assume murder?

"Riley, you ready?"

I jumped, turning to see Maisie zipping her coat.

"Yeah," I squeaked and leaned the broom beside the door inside the kitchen then untied my apron.

"Are we going to tell Agatha about the grimoire tonight?"

"Yep." I froze in the middle of putting my jacket on. "Oh, no." It hit me like a ton of bricks. I had trapped her in the hat and never let her back out. I looked at Maisie, her eyes were as wide as mine. She remembered too. "This is not going to go over well."

I prayed the whole way home that she wasn't still inside the old, floppy witch hat. I hoped she hadn't been trapped inside and was floating around the house, waiting on us to return.

"Agatha?" I called as we walked in the door.

Her hat sat on the kitchen island. Maisie and I exchanged looks. She was not going to be happy. Nope, she was going to be especially upset about this.

"You do it." I pointed to the hat, stepping backward toward the safety of the front door.

Maisie shook her head. "No, you do it! You're the one who trapped her in there!"

"And that's why you should reverse it." I hid around the corner of the entryway, poking my head out with a grimace.

Maisie shook her head. "I'm not going to be the first one she sees! Hell, no!"

Somebody better let me out of this damn hat or I'm going to . . . Agatha's voice echoed in my head, and I knew Maisie had heard it, too, by how she winced.

"Fine," I grumbled to myself and flicked my hand toward the hat. "*Contrarium.*"

A thin twister of black smoke appeared under the hat then vaporized, leaving Agatha standing in its place with the hat on top of her head. Her arms were down by her sides, her hands closed into fists, and her face set into a deep scowl. She looked back and forth between Maisie and me. Pointing a finger at each of us, then said, "Don't ever do that again."

I moved out of my hiding spot; my palms held out. "I didn't mean to—"

She walked toward me with an angry scowl. "I was trapped inside that hat for twenty-eight years. Do you know what that's like? To be trapped for *decades*?"

Her body was becoming opaque. Static saturated the air. I smoothed the strands of hair starting to rise on my head. I had no idea she had been trapped in that hat for so long.

"Who—" I started.

"It doesn't matter." Agatha shook her head. She crossed her arms, rubbing a hand over her upper arm as she stared at the floor.

"It does matter," I argued. "Who trapped you?" I had always wondered why her spirit had been attached to that hat. I figured it had been her own doing, but I had been wrong. Then I thought that maybe Esther had trapped her. They weren't exactly friendly toward one another.

Agatha gazed at me, her body relaxed a bit. The static in the air calmed. "Your mother."

I winced. Why would she do that? What purpose had keeping Agatha's soul around serve her? I wanted to ask, but Maisie cleared her throat. She cocked her head toward my bag still lying next to the arm of the couch from the night before. It was probably best to change the subject. I pulled the large book out, moving closer to Agatha, and hoped she could contain her irritation for a moment longer.

"We found something." Balancing the book in my arms, I pushed open the front cover.

Agatha's mouth opened. "You—" Her fingers solidified and brushed the word *Wildewood*. "Where? How?" She glanced at me and it almost looked like tears were forming in the corner of her eyes. Could ghosts cry? I regarded her long enough for her to turn around. If I didn't know any better, she'd discreetly wiped her eyes.

"Esther—" I began, but Agatha jerked her head toward me.

"Of course." She patted the island counter. "I should've known she had it in her possession this whole time." Agatha then mumbled a few choice words about Madam Mayor before shaking her head.

I laid the book in front of her. She fanned her hand over it and the pages flipped. I had never seen Agatha use magic. I figured it had died along with her physical form.

"I'm not entirely useless," Agatha responded to my thoughts. I hated when she did that.

"Now that we have the grimoire"—Maisie walked to the island—"what now?"

Agatha scowled at her. "Unfortunately, without being able to unlock it, the grimoire itself is useless."

Unlock the book? I frowned, confused.

Her hand stopped moving, and I looked down at the open page. It was blank. I had hoped she would've been able to bring the pages to life, but it seemed even a witch as powerful as she once was couldn't do it.

"Thankfully, you have me. I remember some of what's in this book. So, now, you two will learn how to use your magic."

"We already know how to use our magic." Maisie crossed her arms.

Agatha shook her head and a sharp laugh erupted out of her. "No. You have a very naive understanding of your abilities." She slammed the book closed with a quick swipe of two fingers.

"Naive?" I placed my hands on my hips. "I think we've done a damn good job without anyone teaching us anything."

Agatha thrust her nose into the air, staring at the ceiling. She took a moment, closing her eyes before looking back at me. "All witches have an inherent knowledge of how their magic works. You tapped it. Good for you." She clapped her hand condescendingly. "But you shouldn't have to think about it."

I did have to think about it. After the first "magical happening" I spent weeks trying to figure out how to do it again without any luck. It took me finally stopping and thinking, grounding myself, and allowing that inherent knowledge as she called it, come to the surface for me to perform any of the spells I now knew by heart.

Agatha huffed and threw her hands into the air. "You are Wildewoods, for goodness' sake, and you couldn't even stop a simple spirit."

Agatha's words pierced like a dagger to my heart. She was talking about the possession of Leah Crane. We tried—it wasn't our fault our magic didn't work outside of Wildewood. But she was right. We could've saved Leah before she left the café, but our magic hadn't been strong enough. We didn't know enough.

"Tomorrow, you two will start training." Her image began to quiver. "We should've started a while ago but I was hoping to have the grimoire first. Oh, well. I need to rest up in order to show you how to perform more powerful magic." She snapped her fingers, vanishing into thin air in a puff of black smoke. The gust of wind following her disappearance ruffled my hair.

Oh, goody. I glanced at Maisie, who looked just as excited as I felt. Telling her goodnight, I crawled up the steps to the loft in hopes to sleep away the rest of my hangover.

Chapter 10

I pushed the swinging double doors of the kitchen open with my back, turning slowly so the new batch of blueberry muffins wouldn't fall from the tray. It was early morning, and incredibly busy. Maisie bounced from one customer to another across the café. I could see the stress on her face. Hopefully, this Zachary character would pan out so she could take a breather. Hell, just having another person to handle one side of the café during the rush would be ideal.

The door chimed and the smell of patchouli wrinkled my nose. I had only smelled this perfume on one person—I stilled, almost scared to look. Was Sasha . . . Don't be silly, Riley. I swallowed and saw Jessica Freki. Her face was pale, her cheeks and nose reddened. Her eyes were puffy, and I wondered if she had been crying over the loss of her friend.

I placed the last cupcake into the display case and laid the tray on the counter next to the coffee machine. I grabbed a carafe. "Your usual?"

She wiped at her nose with a tissue. "No, just some tea."

Jessica shoved the used tissue in one pocket then pulled out a clean one from another. She probably had a winter cold. I replaced the carafe and grabbed a packet of honey-lemon tea. There wasn't a large variety of tea to choose from at The Witches Brew, but now that I was trying to get on Officer Russel's good side, I should invest in more flavors. Though, I had a feeling he'd still order "Earl Grey, to go."

I placed a cup of hot water in front of Jessica and handed her the teabag. Last time I had seen her, she had been livid at the Christmas party. Whatever she and the Vargas' had argued about had sent Sasha running away in a fit of tears before she was murdered. Guilt clutched my chest, knowing that was the last time she had seen her friend. "How are you doing?"

She ran the tissue under her nose again. "I'll be all right. It's Manuel I'm worried about. He's not in his right mind."

"I'm sure we'd all feel the same if we lost a spouse."

Jessica snorted, quickly covering her nose with the tissue. "If only that were the reason."

She bobbed the tea bag into the water. Of course, Vargas was upset over his wife's death, right? Jessica placed the plastic lid on her cup. She wiped at her nose again. Or maybe he was upset over the business with Eugene. He certainly wasn't letting up, whatever they were arguing about . . . even with his wife's murderer on the loose.

Jessica looked over her shoulder at the sound of the chime. She slid off her stool and laid a few bucks on the counter. "I gotta go." She rushed past Pete Kelley as he brushed snow off his shoulders. The sun was barely peeking above the treetops, shining through the open blinds of the café.

A timer went off in the kitchen. I hurried to pull the last batch of lemon-blueberry scones out. I would never take advantage of having two working ovens again. I laid the hot tray on the island and fanned myself with the big, gray oven mitt on my hand. I turned the oven off and walked to the back door to crack it open. The soft jingle of a bell echoed through the alley.

"Bean?" I opened the door further and stuck my head out to listen.

Little paw prints littered the fresh snow. I hadn't imagined his presence. Where was he? I stepped into the alley, and something red caught my eye. I walked to the smaller alley between The Witches Brew and the neighboring bookstore. Eugene's toolbox rested against the bricks, buried in a quarter-inch of snow from last night.

I brushed the snow off, and wrapped my fingers around the handle of the toolbox; it was heavier than it looked. I told Maisie I'd be right back then hurried down the street to return it to Eugene before his day began. Without stopping, I reached out to push open the door and smacked my forehead against the glass. Trying the door again, it wouldn't budge. That was weird. The hardware store should be open by now.

Setting the toolbox down, I cupped my hands against the glass and peered into the dark store. I wiped away the fog my breath caused with the sleeve of my sweater.

"Hey, Riley."

I jumped at the sound of Michael's voice behind me. He reached out to push on the door, and I opened my mouth to tell him I had already tried.

"That's weird," he mumbled. "Dad's always here early." He pulled a set of golden keys out of his pocket and unlocked it.

Michael sneezed as we walked into the hardware store. The smell of sawdust wafted around me. It was what I expected to smell whenever I paid a visit, but there was something else lingering I couldn't quite put my finger on. Something wasn't right. The first three rows of shelves were leaning, the shelf in the middle holding them all up. It was teetering, begging to fall under the weight of the others. Michael flicked the light switch on then off, but nothing happened. The hair on the back of my neck stood.

Slivers of soft sunlight poured in from the back and then I noticed the rolling service door wasn't closed all the way. I took a step forward and my boot slipped, sending me to the ground on my butt. Putting my hands down to brace myself, they slipped in something slick. I held them up, and a cry bubbled out of my throat. I looked past the tips of my boots at a trail of blood. I had walked right in it.

I scrambled to my feet, slipping and sliding. There was blood on my jacket and my pants. I looked over at Michael, but his focus was on the ground—on the trail of, what I could only assume, was his father's blood.

He finally snapped his jaw shut, looking at me. "You need to get out of here." He took a step toward me.

I moved back, almost losing my balance. "What?" Where was I going to go? I was a part of the crime scene.

Michael raised his voice, telling me to leave again, and I burst into tears. I stopped myself from touching my face, my hands wet with blood.

Michael's shoulders tensed; his jaw tight. He ran a hand over his face. "Call the police." Carefully, he walked around the pool of blood toward the back. The snow from the morning had blown into the building and had turned a shade of brown from mixing with the blood. "I was never here." He jerked his head in my direction.

"What?" My heart began to race.

"Riley. You never saw me. I was never here." He took a long step over the bloody snow. "I cannot be here when they come."

"I don't understand!" I cried out, but Michael vanished, slipping out the open service door. I looked around, feeling stunned. What was he hiding from? He had been just as shocked as I had when we walked into the store. He hadn't done this, so why was he running?

With my feet wanting to slip out from under me, I carefully walked to the register and picked up the phone. I dialed 9-1-1 and recognized Suzie's voice on the other end. She was one of Wildewood's only operators.

"Hey, Suz." I sniffled. "Something really bad happened at Fletchers Hardware." I choked back a cry. "Something really bad."

I lowered the phone back into the cradle, leaving a bloody handprint wrapped around it. I faced the store, taking in the scene. What happened here? Who would want to hurt Eugene? I sniffled, needing to wipe my nose desperately. Did this have to do with the argument between Eugene and Vargas? Without getting blood on my face, I used my upper arm to wipe at the snot draining from my nose. I sucked in a deep breath and whimpered.

I didn't want to move. I didn't want to mess anything else up. So, I stared at the service door instead. My eyes trailed the drag marks. Had Eugene been attacked and dragged out of the store? He was a big guy, a real big guy. I couldn't think of one person in this town who could overtake a man the size, and presumed strength, of Eugene.

Something under one of the shelves that had fallen over caught my attention. I took a step but stopped. Don't make it

worse, I reminded myself. I lowered on my haunches and leaned
closer, using only my fingertips to keep me balanced. There was
something purple. It almost looked like a flower petal.

I jumped up when the front door opened.

John Russell walked in with his nose wrinkled, stifling a
sneeze. His eyes landed on me, looking me over from head to
toe. I lowered my head. This was not going to do anything for
our relationship. No amount of tea would help him overlook
this mistake.

Chapter 11

Hours later, I sat beside Pete's desk in a pair of dark-blue sweats with "WPD" in bold, white letters across the chest and down the left pant leg. Suzie gave me a pair of bright-yellow flip-flops she had in her car that were at least two sizes too big.

I stared into the watered-down coffee I held with both hands in my lap. After taking a print of my boots, one of the investigators had offered them back to me . . . but they were trash. The thought of trying to scrub the blood from them turned my stomach. I did not want them back. I didn't want my clothes back either, though no one had offered.

Pete's desk shook as he plopped into his seat. He scooted closer and placed his own cup of coffee cup that said "World's Greatest Cop" in front of him. He ripped off the tops of three sugar packets and sprinkled them into the liquid then stirred it with a plastic spoon.

"Okay." He pulled out his little notebook from his chest pocket and clicked his pen. "One more time . . ."

I had already told him what I'd seen, what I'd done. I told him, Russell, and another officer separately. He had my statement written down in front of him. I sighed, lifting the coffee to my lips. I forced myself to swallow the tepid liquid.

"I was returning Eugene's toolbox. He left it at The Witches Brew."

Pete scribbled. "And why was he there?"

I tried to stop it, but I huffed. He had already written this down. "He was fixing my ovens."

Pete looked at me, a weak smile gracing his lips. "I am so glad they got it fixed. You know I can't go a morning without one of your—"

A throat cleared. Pete's smile vanished. I looked over my shoulder to see Officer Russell with a perpetual frown standing behind me. I was starting to think that look had nothing to do with my muffins or coffee. I think it was just his face.

"How did you get in the store?" Pete continued.

This is where I started to lie and I really, really, hated lying. "It was unlocked." My hands started to shake. I gripped the cup a little tighter and felt the Styrofoam starting to give under my nails.

"Did you see Michael?" Russell pulled a chair out to sit in front of me.

I shook my head. A strand of hair fell in front of my eye and I took my hand off the cup for just a second to push it back behind my ear. Closing my eyes, I repeated what I wrote on the yellow legal pad sitting in front of Pete.

"I walked in. The shelves were toppled over and then I slipped on—" Stomach acid burned my throat and tears stung my eyes.

Pete put his notebook down and patted my knee. "He's a tough guy."

A tear slipped down my cheek and I wiped it away as quickly as I could. Russell handed his business card to me. "I know your boyfriend and Michael are friends. If he shows up, you call me."

I took the card and stared at the number. I hadn't even realized he and Ethan were friends. I knew they knew each other but . . . this was just one more thing I didn't know about Ethan.

"Can I go?" I asked.

Russell stood, pushing his chair back under his desk. "Riley." He took the drink from my hands, shocking me with a little zap of static electricity. "I'm serious. Call me if you see Michael."

I nodded. "Is he in trouble?"

"Not yet." Russell showed me to the door.

I stepped out of the station, the cold air gripping me tight. Flip-flops and snow did not mix well but I was so glad I had something on my feet. I debated on whether or not to just go home, but I knew Maisie was probably worried sick. I had been in such a state of shock, I hadn't even thought of calling her. I looked behind me, through the glass door of the police station. I could go back in and use the phone, but I had just lied to Officer Russell and wanted to be as far away from him as possible.

My toes were frozen by the time I stepped into the café. Maisie looked up from the register, her jaw dropped as I approached her. "What happened? Pete called a while ago. He said you were okay. What happened to your clothes?" she asked.

Thank God for Pete.

I shook my head, and overheard someone ask, "Has anyone seen Michael?"

Sure have, I thought, fleeing a crime scene. But what was Michael running from? If he had nothing to do with . . . whatever happened to his father then why didn't he stick around? He had been very adamant about not being there when the cops showed up, I just didn't understand why.

"I cannot believe someone would hurt Eugene," another person whispered, and it caused my stomach to twist and tears stung my eyes. Sometimes I really hated how fast word spread in this town.

They were right, though. Who would want to hurt him?

I sat on an empty stool in front of the counter.

Vargas. He had been arguing with Eugene at Town Hall and outside the hardware store. Eugene's disappearance had to do with whatever 'business' they were involved in together. But what was it? Was it something to kill over? A soft whimper escaped me. He couldn't be dead. He was only missing, right?

A hand touched my shoulder, and I almost jumped out of my skin. Ethan held his hands up, palms facing out. "Whoa. You okay?" His eyes roamed over me. "Where did you get those clothes from?"

Maisie whispered to him, explaining what had happened and Ethan's eyes widened. He sat on the stool beside me, swiveling mine to face him. "You okay?"

I nodded because that's all I felt I could do.

Maisie cleared her throat. "Do either of you want some coffee? I'm sure we have some left."

It was almost time for the café to close for the afternoon. Normally, I would never turn down a cup of coffee, but right now all I wanted to do was wake up from this nightmare. Without bringing too much attention to myself, I pinched my arm. When I didn't spring up in my bed, I sighed. This wasn't a dream, just a real-life nightmare.

"Does Michael know?" Ethan pressed his hand to my back, rubbing in small, gentle circles.

I swallowed, not wanting to lie to him, too. "Yes. He knows."

"I'm going to go see if he's okay." Ethan pulled his cell phone from his pocket, placed a kiss on my temple then rushed out of the café.

But he wasn't going to be able to find his friend. Michael was hiding. I just didn't understand why.

Chapter 12

Maisie walked with me back home so I could change into some clothes that fit me. My toes were freezing, and I desperately wanted a shower. But as we walked past the hardware store, my steps faltered. Her hand found mine and I looked down to see our matching crescent-moon birthmarks right below our thumbs.

Bean had the same marking between his eyes. I wonder where he was hiding. It wasn't like him to be gone this long. I had no doubt he could take care of himself; I was fairly certain he was a lot older than the average cat. Though how old, I had no idea.

The police tape over the front door fluttered in the wind, taunting us as if it were about to fly away at any moment. We rounded the street corner, the flimsy flip-flops on my feet slipping on the snow. Maisie hooked her arm in mine to help steady me. I caught a glimpse of more bright-yellow police tape blocking off the alley behind the hardware store.

"What happened here?" Maisie pulled me toward the alley.

The crime scene tape went from each edge of the building to the fence that blocked our alley from the neighboring one.

The snow had been manipulated by the crime scene investigators, and any indication of what might have happened, erased.

"I don't know." And that was the truth. I had no idea what happened to Eugene. I had no idea if he was alive or not. Someone had hurt him and dragged his body out of the hardware store. The trail of blood made that evident.

I was compiling quite a long list of I don't knows between Sasha's murder and whatever happened with Eugene.

As soon as we got home, I tossed the flip-flops off and went straight to the shower. With only a towel around me, I ran up the stairs. I threw the WPD sweats toward the hamper between the dresser and the wall. They fell short and landed on the edge of the dresser. Grabbing a white crew-neck shirt, I couldn't stop thinking about the purple petal I saw under one of the fallen shelves. Something about it bothered me. It looked similar to the flowers that had been in the bathroom at Town Hall and I wondered if the police noticed it, too.

The floor of the hardware store was usually littered with sawdust and other debris. Eugene was an excellent handyman, but his store wasn't swept very often. If it weren't for me slipping, I'm not sure I would've noticed it.

Then there was that smell, something very subtle among the scent of sawdust and metal. Had the police smelled it? I pulled on a pair of black jeggings and thick winter socks. I could have imagined it, I suppose. I know I had smelled that scent before, but it had been so subtle I was having trouble putting my finger on it.

Going to my closet, I looked at the few pairs of shoes neatly lined up on the floor and sighed. I loved my boots. I grabbed a newer pair that did not have that worn-in feeling and crammed my feet in.

With a clean, white, crew-neck shirt on and a thin, black-and-white, buffalo-plaid flannel on top, I walked back down the stairs to see Maisie sitting at the kitchen table. The blinds had been pulled up and she was staring outside. Large, fluffy snow-flakes drifted to the ground, replacing the snow from the previous night that had already melted under the late-morning sun.

I fully expected Agatha to appear at any moment. But she was still "resting," whatever that meant for a ghost. And I honestly wasn't upset about it. I didn't have the energy to banter with her. I slumped in the chair to the left of Maisie and she pushed a sandwich in front of me.

We had decided a few weeks ago that we needed to add another food group to our diets. Apparently, it wasn't 'healthy' to live on cocoa rice crispies. But neither of us enjoyed cooking after work. So, sandwiches it was. They weren't as good as Mike's club sandwiches, but that was on the other side of town.

I brought the plate closer to me and stared at it. I wasn't hungry. I wasn't feeling much of anything. Glancing from the sandwich to Maisie, I poked her in the arm.

"Sorry." She shook her head as if it brought her attention away from whatever she had been staring at outside. "This is just crazy. First Sasha, and now Eugene. What the hell is going on in this town?"

I leaned against the table with my elbow and blinked lazily as I tried to formulate an answer. I remember Michael telling his father that "nothing's changed." But he was wrong, something had changed and it was darkening Wildewood. I had an inkling it had something to do with us.

I brought the sandwich to my lips, deciding I would probably regret not eating later. I kept my eyes on her as I took a bite. I wasn't going to worry her just yet. Maisie had a hard exterior but she also had a tendency to get worked up when she felt scared. No need to panic her. Not yet.

Anyway, we had a new employee to train and I needed one of us to be focused because right now, my mind felt as if it were a million miles away.

Chapter 13

Z ach rubbed the back of his neck, staring at the scribble on the ticket Maisie handed him. "What's the Rich Witch, again?"

The corners of her lips twitched. She tapped her fingers to her mouth to hide it. Scooting closer to him, she pointed at the cheat sheet she'd made lying on the counter. "You start with drizzling caramel in the bottom of the cup." Maisie reached past him, her arm rubbing against his, to grab the container and handed it to him. Smooth, Mais. "Fill it with the cold brew, then top it with whipped topping, then drizzle more caramel on top."

He nodded and followed her directions. "Okay. Got it." He held up the coffee drink, a drop of caramel running down the side, for her approval. Her eyes lit up as she smiled. Zach slipped around the counter with the drink in hand to deliver it.

Maisie's cheeks were flushed, and I cracked a grin. I had never seen her smitten before. I wonder if that's how I'd looked the first time I saw Ethan? On second thought, I'm fairly certain I looked like a boiled lobster.

Zach walked back to the bar, and I caught her stealing a

glance at him. I decided to leave the two of them alone, also I was feeling a little creepy staring at the potential blossoming relationship. Swerving around the café with a tray, I gathered up empty dishes. I started walking toward the kitchen when a shadowy movement caught my attention.

I set the tray behind the counter and watched it move under the swinging doors. Pushing them open, I bumped into something large and fell backward onto my butt. Looking up, Zach stared down at me. I glanced past his legs, searching the kitchen. The fluorescent lights brightened every corner, pushing out any hiding spot for whatever the shadow was.

"Looking for something?" Zach asked. He wrapped his hand around mine and pulled me back up to my feet.

"I thought I saw—" I shook my head and dusted my backside off. "Never mind."

But I knew I had seen it again. The little shadowy creature. It had been helpful with finding the grimoire, but what was it still doing lurking around?

The door chimed, and I looked over my shoulder. Tessa smiled and waved at me. I wiped my hands on my apron and met her at the counter where she perched on a stool. Washing the floor from my hands, I dried them quickly, then poured her a cup of coffee. "How'd the sale go?"

"Got rid of a lot of bags." Her smile faded and her eyes grew with concern. "I heard what happened at the hardware store." She reached across the counter and touched my arm. "I am so sorry you keep—" She twisted her lips.

Finding dead people? Trampling through crime scenes? Yeah, me too. "It's okay. I just hope they figure out what's going on, and quick." But if Vargas had anything to do with it, as I suspect

74

he did Eugene's case, I wasn't sure we would ever find out what really happened.

"Who's that?" Tessa nodded toward Zach.

"Zachary Osbourne. He just started tonight." I watched as he picked up a dirty cup and saucer. "I think we're going to keep him."

Tessa chuckled. "He's not a pet, Riley." She placed a gift bag on the counter. "You forgot Ethan's gift."

I pressed my lips tight together to stifle a chuckle as Zach handed me the dirty dishes.

"Hey." Tessa wiggled her fingers and accidentally knocked her spoon on the ground. "Whoops." She fluttered her lashes at Zach. "Could you get that for me?"

I rubbed my temple, trying hard not to laugh at how obvious Tessa was being. Zach bent over, his shirt slightly pulling up to expose skin right above his belt. Tessa looked at me and wiggled her eyebrows. Oh, good grief. I placed my hand over my mouth. She was too much some days.

Zach straightened up, spoon in hand. "Let me get you a new one."

I rolled my eyes at Tessa as Zach began to hand Tessa a new spoon, but he tucked his arm back to his side. "Actually, this one has a spot on it." He placed it in the sink and with a napkin, he picked up another one and placed it on the table beside her cup, crumpling the napkin up, then sliding it into his apron.

One of the last customers called him over.

I crossed my arms, tilting my head to look at Tessa. "What was that all about?"

Tessa picked up the spoon. "I was hoping to get a read off of him. But"—she placed the spoon back on the counter with a shrug—"he never touched the spoon." She took a sip of her coffee. "Have you guys gotten your tree yet?"

Flicking my eyes to the ceiling, I shook my head. There were only ten days left until Christmas. At this rate, we should just wait until next year.

"Well, there's a little place right on the edge of town, before the bridge, called Peaceful Acres. They sell Christmas trees."

What Tessa was really saying was to get a move on before we ran out of time. She picked up her coffee and blew me a kiss before turning to leave. I padded into my office and set Ethan's present on the desk. I wasn't even sure the camera worked, but it looked vintage and that was cool, right? Was it too late to order matching outfits for everyone?

I walked to the front door, my fingers stilling as I watched Ethan hop the fence of the patio. He looked up and our eyes met. He winked, his smile deepening as my cheeks turned red. I took a step back as he opened the door. He leaned down to press his lips against mine, causing my eyes to flutter closed, his vanilla scent tightening things low in my body.

I opened my eyes when his lips pulled away. He was staring past me, so I glanced over my shoulder.

"I see you finally hired someone."

Zach leaned over to wipe down a table. The muscles in his arm flexed under the white crew-neck shirt. His apron purposely twisted to the side. It looked much smaller on him than it did on Maisie or me. I looked back at Ethan, a sly smile on my lips.

"Jealous?"

He shook his head, his honey-colored locks moving freely. He pressed his lips against mine again, this time not as gentle, his arm slipped around my back and he pulled me against him. He lowered his mouth to my ear and whispered, "Not at all."

Out of the corner of my eye, I saw Zach glance at Ethan. It wasn't the friendliest look, though it only lasted a split second before he busied himself with a spot on the table in front of him. Did Zach recognize him? Ethan didn't seem to know him. I patted Ethan's chest and walked to the register to take out the till.

"I'm almost ready to get out of here," I said, counting one-dollar bills and scribbling the total on a scrap piece of paper.

Ethan came up beside me, helping himself to the remaining bit of coffee. "I'm not in much of a rush." He pressed against my back, wrapping his arms around my waist.

"Not much of a rush?" I stopped counting, hoping I wouldn't lose my place.

His lips brushed my neck before he walked back around the counter to sit in front of me. I blinked stupidly at him for a moment, my neck tingling where his lips had touched. "I developed that film you found."

That piqued my interest and I lost my place. Who was I kidding, it had been lost the second Ethan touched me. Grabbing the wad of fives, I started again.

"Did you say you found it at Tessa's?"

"Mhmm." I nodded my head, not taking my eyes off the money in front of me, otherwise, we'd never get to leave.

"I'm interested to see what you think of the pictures." Ethan tapped the counter rhythmically.

Crap. What number was I on? Sixty-five, I think. Or was it seventy-five? Shit. I placed the pile down and gave Ethan my most angelic smile.

"Sorry." He pressed his lips together in a thin line. "I'll go."
He looked behind him. "I'll wait outside."

"You don't have to do that. It's freezing outside." I felt bad,
but damn if he wasn't distracting.

Ethan chuckled. "I'll be fine."

Chapter 14

We dropped Maisie off before heading to Ethan's house. He lived on the next street past ours. He parked the old pick-up truck and I climbed out, following him under the car-port and into the mudroom outside of the kitchen. His house had a bachelor feel. Minimal decor. A large acrylic painting of a wolf howling at the moon hung over a navy-blue couch. A flat-screen TV, triple the size of mine.

I laid my jacket on the arm of the couch and pulled my shoes off. My pinkie toes sighed in relief. These boots just weren't the same as the old ones. I padded over to the kitchen. Ethan opened the refrigerator and pulled out two beers, handing me one. I frowned and stuck out my tongue. I didn't want to taste or smell alcohol again for a very long time.

Ethan's eyes creased in amusement. "How 'bout a water?"

"That sounds better."

He handed me a cold water bottle, popped the lid off his beer, then led me to the darkroom. Ushering me in, he shut the door behind us and flipped a red light on. It took my eyes a moment to adjust to the strange lighting. As my eyes dilated, I saw a couple of pictures hanging by clothespins on the opposite end.

"I didn't understand why Tessa wanted you to see what's on the film, but . . ." Ethan walked past me and unclipped one of the photos. I took it from him, making note of how attentively he was watching me as I brought it closer. "I can see the resemblance. Is it a relative?"

My breath caught in my throat. I choked back a cry. A wave of dizziness rushed over me. The picture slipped from my hand as I reached out to grab onto something, anything to hold me steady. Ethan wrapped his hands around my arms.

"What just happened, Riley? Are you okay?"

Tears hovered in my eyes, clouding my vision as I looked up to meet his stare. I never told him what Tessa told me. I never mentioned that the film had a familiar feel, or that it was my mother's memories. I figured Tessa was wrong. She had to be wrong because why would anything belonging to a woman who had been dead for almost three decades end up in her store?

Then again, Agatha ended up there.

Ethan picked the picture off the floor. "Do you recognize her?"

Taking in a shaky breath, I touched the woman's face in the picture. My fingers trailed down her arm to the bundles in her lap. "She's my mother," my voice was so soft, I wasn't even sure I had said it out loud.

"Your mother?"

I just knew it was. She looked so much like me, even though the picture was in black and white. We had the same features, the same square jawline. We even had the same smile. Confusion rushed over me. She was smiling. How could that be? We were given up. How could she be smiling while holding us when we were abandoned shortly afterward? A tear slipped down my cheek and landed on the picture. Drying it with my shirt, I looked at Ethan. His features were serious, brows creased, as he brushed my cheek, wiping away another tear.

"Are you sure?" he asked.

I nodded. Sitting next to her was Bean. The white patch between his eyes in the shape of a crescent moon gave him away. This was her, there was no doubt in my mind. "What's on the other pictures?" my voice quivered.

"They're mostly the same." He unclipped the rest and handed them to me.

I shuffled through the pile. In half of the pictures, the flash hadn't been on and they were dark. I flipped through them again and something caught my attention. In the bottom corner, though it was dark, I could just barely make out a shape. "Can you enlarge this?"

Ethan looked down where my finger was. "Enlarge what?"

I pointed to the spot. "I know it looks like nothing is there, but could you humor me? Please?"

"Yeah." His eyes roamed my face for a moment. "Yeah, I can." Ethan took the photo from me to hang back up with the clothespin. "It's nothing more than just a shadow though."

It wasn't just a shadow. It was *the* shadow. The one I had seen a few times recently. If I could see it better, it might be possible to figure out what it was. If I knew what it was, maybe I could figure out why it was following me around.

I picked out the first picture he had given me. "Can I keep this?"

"Of course. They're yours." He gave me a half-smile and wrapped one of his large hands around mine then led me out of the darkroom. "Are you sure you're okay?"

I nodded, but even I didn't believe it. I was just sick of being asked if I was okay. It was a lot to take in, and it would take more than a few seconds to be okay. I had never seen what my mother looked like. I figured she resembled Agatha, the same way Maisie did. But no. My mother and I favored one another, and it was so strange to finally put a face to her name.

Ethan took the picture from my hands and set it down on top of my jacket. "You look spooked."

No, not spooked. Speechless. Confused. Even with Tessa's warning, I had not expected this. A picture of my mother holding us. I wonder how soon after she abandoned us? I didn't know how to feel. I wanted to cry. I wanted to be happy that I finally knew what she looked like. But then I was angry that she was smiling in the picture. Agatha said she would've been a good mother, that it was her magic that consumed her.

I was feeling so many things at once and then I caught Ethan watching me.

The golden ring around his irises had grown, the blue shrinking away. He lowered his head to mine, his lips gently touching me as if he were afraid I would break. I grabbed his shirt and pulled him closer. At this point, I didn't care if I shattered. I pressed myself against his lean, muscular form, unable to get enough of him. His hands roamed down my back, cupping my bottom and picking me up. I wrapped my legs around his waist and he carried me down the hall to his bedroom.

Chapter 15

I pulled the thread-barren, charcoal-gray comforter over my body and rolled onto my stomach. With my arms crossed under my head, I watched Ethan. His eyes were closed, his arms behind his head against the headboard. His chest rose and fell evenly. The corner of his mouth twitched into a smirk as he opened one eye to catch me staring.

He slid down, turning to rest on his side with his head propped on his fist. His fingers trailed over my shoulder. "What's on your mind, beautiful?" He pressed his lips over the goose-bumps his fingers left.

"You." I pushed my hair behind an ear. "Your secrets."

His fingers hesitated for a second. "What secrets?"

Narrowing my eyes at him for just a second, I responded, "Your issue with Esther, for instance."

His forehead creased. He looked at me and the expression was gone. "I don't have an issue with her."

Sitting up, I pressed the comforter tightly against my chest. "You get grumpy whenever she's around and she's—"

"A bully."

He moved back to lean against the headboard with his arms crossed over his chest. The sheet pooled in his lap, leaving little to the imagination. I moved my focus up his body, over his chiseled pecs, his muscular arms, and rested on his lips. Biting the inside of my cheek, I pondered what he'd said. I knew Esther could be demanding. But a bully? I'm not sure I'd go that far. Well, maybe borderline bully.

Okay—she did occasionally dip her toes into bully territory. But she usually had a reason.

Ethan stared across the room. His blue eyes focused, deep in thought. I toyed with the idea of pushing the conversation further, but the stern look on his face made me reconsider. He could say nothing was going on between them all he wanted, but I knew that to not be true. He spoke in grunts and growls when he had to interact with her. It had me wondering what she knew about him, or vice-a-versa.

But, if he didn't want to talk about it, then I'd change the subject.

"Were you able to find Michael?"

He shook his head. His fingers combed his hair back away from his face. "Not yet."

"I hope you find him soon." And I really did. Michael running off the way he did had me concerned over what he was running from.

Ethan leaned over, the serious look slowly melting away, and kissed my temple. "Did you tell me you and Maisie had something to do tonight?"

His words caused me to recoil. Was he kicking me out?

I turned my back to him, leaning over the bed to grab my clothes off the floor. I could take a hint. He didn't want to talk, fine. We wouldn't talk. If I wanted to, I could use the same spell on him that I use on Pete when I needed information. But I had promised myself I would never do that. I didn't want to have to force him to open up—a girl had to have some standards—but he was making it obvious he didn't want to let me in.

I would just have to figure out what was going on between them my own way.

The bed rocked slightly. A moment later, Ethan stood in front of me, wearing only his boxer briefs. He handed me my pants and I resisted the urge to snatch them out of his hand. Instead, I took them like a mature adult and slipped them on as I stood.

"I'm not kicking you out, Riley."

I walked out of the room to grab my belongings. Pulling my jacket on, I folded the picture in half and slid it into a pocket.

Ethan grabbed my wrist, turning me to face him. "Don't be mad."

I wriggled my arm free. "I'm not mad." Nope, not at all. Not one tiny iota of anger, but of course I was lying. "I just wish you'd let me in some. You know everything about me."

I stiffened as he wrapped his arms around me. "Riley, I—" He snapped his jaw shut, searching my face. "Do you want me to drive you home?"

"No." I slid my feet into the uncomfortable boots, not bothering to tie them. "I'll see you later." I walked past him and stepped into the cold night, shutting the door behind me before he had a chance to follow.

The snowfall had picked up. The large fluffy flakes dampened my jacket and hair. A shiver ran down my spine, and I pulled my hood up. Reconsidering his offer, I glanced back at the house, the lights in the living room had already been turned off.

Nope. I would not give him the satisfaction. I just needed to walk off my irritation and hopefully tomorrow it wouldn't bother me so much. But, dammit! It hurt that he kept shutting me out. Rolling my eyes, I remembered I still had to deal with Agatha.

I stomped on to Cattail Road, my shoelaces slapping the ground, the sound loud on the quiet street and then a howl stopped me in my tracks. I stood under the weak light of a lamppost, my breathing growing rapidly. The hair on the back of my neck stood. Another wolf answered the first. I turned in a circle and screamed as something large ran past me.

My coat fanned away from my body as it moved out of sight so fast I couldn't make out what it was. Heart racing, hands shaking; had it been a wolf? Were there wolves in Wildewood? Not wanting to find out, I started to run, and another howl echoed.

New plan! There was no way in Hell I was going to run home while wolves were so close. I grabbed my keys and unhooked the little broom. My house was only another five minutes on foot, but I was not going to end up a midnight snack for these creatures.

"*Crescere*," I whispered, hoping nothing could hear me. I was taking a chance at my neighbors seeing, but I had bigger problems to worry about right now.

The broom teetered in my hand, shaking as it grew in size until I could no longer palm it.

I swung my leg over the handle. "*Subvolare*," I spoke magic into the broom, allowing it to get me the hell out of dodge.

Rising into the air, I made a sharp turn and cut above the trees to head straight toward my backyard. Hopefully, the large, wooden privacy fence would keep whatever was stalking me out. I hovered above the trees and forced the broom to turn in a slow circle. I caught a glimpse of two very large—I mean, unnaturally large—wolves heading into a thick patch of trees. I knew we lived in the middle of a forest; I knew there had to be animals around us. It was sort of a given, but I had never seen one up close.

The wolves howled in unison, and I jumped, pulling the broom upward. Unfortunately, my jump caused the broom to move vertically and I began to slide down the handle. I had never had my broom flip upside down before and the more I struggled, the worse it became.

"*Demittere!*" I screamed for it to lower.

The broom only budged a few inches toward the ground. My legs dangled a dangerous height above the porch, I gripped the handle tight as it completely turned over, back to horizontal, but without me on top.

"*Demittere!*" I repeated and dropped down a foot. I tried to pull it down, but the magic of the broom was stronger than my ability to do a pull-up. "Lower, now, you asshole!"

The broom fell. My feet landed on the porch. My knees bent under the impact and I fell forward, barely catching myself in time before my nose hit the ground.

Pushing myself into a sitting position and glowering at the broom, I stood on achy knees and laid it against the house next to the back door. I had no idea what that was about, how that had even happened. I would make sure in the future that I didn't clutch the handle in a hug, no matter how freaked out I was. I had been lucky not to be so high up. I wiped the snow off my knees then walked into the house.

In the kitchen, Maisie looked up from the table, a big smile on her face. "Look who came back!" She turned, so I could see Bean curled up in her lap.

I let out a sigh of relief, it was so good to see him. Especially after witnessing what was running around Wildewood.

Chapter 16

I rubbed under Bean's chin. He raised his head, eyes shut tight, and began to purr. I knew he could take care of himself, but there were wolves in Wildewood and he was just a little cat. There was no way he could protect himself against an animal so large. Well, I assumed. He wasn't an average cat, so maybe he could take on a wolf.

"You look a little spooked." Maisie handed Bean to me as she stood.

"Yeah, a little." I nuzzled his warm body. "There are wolves running around."

She stood in front of the open refrigerator door and looked over her shoulder. "Wolves?" She pushed the door shut with her hip, a gallon of milk in one hand. "You sure?"

How had she not heard the howls? They had been so close, basically in our backyard. "Positive. They're probably just trying to find some food now that it's December," I reassured, probably myself more than anyone.

I set Bean on the ground and pulled the folded picture out

of my jacket pocket. I tossed the jacket on the chair closest to me and laid the photo on the table.

"What's this?" Maisie placed a bowl of cocoa crispies in front of me before she picked the picture up.

Through a mouth full of cereal, I asked, "Do you remember that roll of film I found at Tessa's?"

Maisie unfolded the photo. She looked up at me for a moment, before her eyes returned to what I could only assume was our mother's face. "Is this who I think it is?" she whispered.

Before I could answer, Agatha materialized behind her. "Where did you get that?" She grabbed at the picture, but her hand moved through it.

I swallowed, the cereal scratching my throat as it went down.

Agatha reached for the picture again, her hand hesitated. "Ya know,"—she crossed her arms, a finger tapping against her lip—"she could've been a great mother if . . ." She stared at the picture, her eyes distant as if she was lost in a memory.

"If what?" I pushed the bowl away.

"If her power hadn't consumed her." Agatha waved her hand and the grimoire floated from the living room to the kitchen island. "Too bad this thing is useless." With a flick of her wrist, the book opened to the middle. The pages were still blank. She motioned with her fingers and the pages flipped to more empty pages. "We're still missing the key to its knowledge." She flicked her wrist and the book slammed shut. "Nevertheless, I still retain all the knowledge I died with."

"Why are the pages blank?" I asked, reopening the empty book. My fingers tingled as they trailed over the old pages. The book was ripe with magic, from generations of witches, even if we couldn't see what had once been written. Magic oozed from its spine as if it possessed the magic of each witch before us.

"In a way, it does," Agatha answered.

I glared at her. I did not like when she intruded into my thoughts. "How?"

"Every Wildewood witch has used this book to learn and harness their power. It's unfortunate you two are starting so . . ." She shrugged.

"Starting so late? So old? You know we're only twenty-eight. You're what . . . in your mid-fifties?" I refrained from sticking my tongue out.

"What I mean is, I was using complicated spells by the time I was ten. All you can do is simple commands. It's a pity." She clicked her tongue and waved me out of the way. Her hands solidified for a moment as her fingertips touched the page. A look of nostalgia washed over her, but she shook her head and closed the book.

It wasn't our fault we were abandoned as infants and lived outside of Wildewood our entire life. We hadn't been given the opportunity to spend the last twenty-eight years learning magic. The fault rested on our mother's shoulders, and, sometimes I think, Esther Miller. I had this suspicion she was behind us not being adopted or raised within Wildewood. Though, it was only a suspicion. I didn't know what happened to our mother or why we were given up. Our father hadn't known about us, but I know if he had, he would've raised us and we wouldn't be newbies when it came to our magic.

"Follow me." Agatha floated toward the stairs. "Bring a few pencils." She snapped her fingers and the junk drawer in the island opened.

"This ought to be interesting," Maisie mumbled, grabbing a handful of unsharpened pencils.

We ran to catch up with Agatha, and then she floated through the back door. "She forgot to mention we were going outside." I ran back into the kitchen and grabbed my jacket from the table, and Maisie's hanging beside the front door.

Stepping out into the cold, we put our coats on.

Agatha lectured us about an attack spell. "*Percutio.*" She waved her hand, and one of the pencils Maisie was still clutching flew toward a tree in the backyard. "It's a way to turn any object into a projectile."

"What exactly are you wanting us to do?" I asked, glancing at Maisie as she put the pencils on the snow-covered railing.

"You two need to learn how to protect yourselves. This is a rather simple incantation." Agatha waved her hand and the pencils rose in the air. One by one she laid them back on the railing. "I assume you already know how to make things float." Agatha moved back; her hands held behind her back.

I held my hand out toward one of the pencils. "*Surgere.*" The pencil rose a foot into the air. "*Demittere.*" I lowered my hand and the pencil laid back in its original spot. I glanced over my shoulder, at my broom, as if it needed its own lesson on how to behave.

"Good. Now, make the pencil rise and then recite the new spell. Aim toward that tree." She pointed toward the closest tree, near the back of the fence where her pencil was embedded in the bark.

Maisie nodded toward me. "You first."

I lifted my hand, the pencil rising back into the air. I reared my arm back, and as I threw my hand forward, I spoke the new word, "*Percutio*." The pencil barreled into the trunk of the tree. I smirked. Easy peasy.

Maisie did the same, her pencil sticking out right above mine.

Agatha clapped her hands, which barely made any noise. "Okay, now do it without the command word." She crossed her arms, narrowing her eyes at me and my arrogance.

"Easy," I muttered. I extended my hand again. I had used this spell enough with my broom that I rarely had to say it. The broken, yellow pencil rose into the air and, as if throwing a ball, I threw the pencil toward the tree. The pencil only shook then fell below the porch. Okay—that was rather anticlimactic. I leaned over the railing to see it sticking out of the snow. It's fine. Try again, Riley. No one could do this on their first try. Rolling my shoulders back, I brought it back into the air in front of me and begged it to hit the tree but it fell again. I looked at Maisie and she shrugged. "It's because I've never used this spell before."

Agatha shook her head, rolling her eyes. "Maisie, your turn."

Maisie flung the pencil without uttering a word. It pierced the trunk of the tree in an explosion of bark as it buried itself to the eraser. My mouth gaped. How the hell had she done that so easily?

"Good, Maisie." Agatha turned her attention to me. "You shouldn't need to recite the command words. You should know it, understand it, and just do it. No words needed."

Maisie's grin touched her eyes until she saw me then it faded quickly. "Beginner's luck? I probably couldn't do it again." But she did—a second pencil split the first one.

I wasn't so sure this was beginner's luck. We both came into our powers around the same time. I stole a glance at Agatha, she was watching Maisie. Her brows creased, creating a deep line between her eyes. I remember what Tessa had told us when we learned about the Wildewood witches: One of us would become corrupt with power. Maisie was the stronger of us, I had known that from the very first moment I saw her use her magic, and this cleared up any doubt in my mind. Was Maisie in danger of her own power? Would she end up like our mother? I caught Agatha looking at me and she nodded, barely but enough for me to notice. She was worried too.

Agatha dismissed us but I stayed outside trying over and over until I finally was able to hit my target. It was exhausting and my ego was bruised. Could it really be just beginner's luck that Maisie was able to do this spell without saying a word? Magic came so easy to her.

I grabbed the remaining pencils and walked into the warm house.

I threw the pencils back into the drawer. The shower turned off and I hurried upstairs. I didn't want to talk about it with her just yet. Hopefully, and I really did hope, it was nothing more than a fluke. But deep in my gut, I knew Maisie truly was stronger and the way Agatha had looked at her, the worry she tried to conceal, let me know I wasn't wrong. She thought it too.

I kicked off my shoes and laid down, staring at the ceiling. Bean jumped on the edge of the bed and circled into a ball. Rolling over, I ran my hand down his soft, black coat. "We have to keep an eye on her," I whispered, and he began to purr.

I started to doze off. My thoughts wandered from Maisie to the secrets Ethan was keeping from me then to the inside of the hardware store. My eyes opened as Bean jumped to the floor. I listened to his paws pad down the steps.

Changing into pajamas, I crawled under the covers and decided I was going to figure out if the petal hidden under the fallen shelves was important or not. However, the way I planned to go about finding this out some might consider illegal. We would have to be sneaky. It would have to be done before Wildewood woke up. And I knew Maisie wasn't going to be too thrilled.

Chapter 17

"Oh, God!" Maisie screamed in my ear. Her arms were wrapped uncomfortably tight around my waist. "I hate this so much!" she hissed, her arms tightening to get her point across.

I laughed. "It's not that bad!"

Maisie's arms loosened, and I took a deep breath. She jabbed a finger into my side.

Since the last time we'd flown together, Maisie had vocalized her extreme dislike of riding a broom as a means of transportation, or maybe it was just riding it together. I couldn't argue with her, because the last time we almost died. It was possible her fear wasn't completely irrational . . . the keyword was *almost*. I rode my broom all the time and only once—okay, now twice—I'd had a bad experience.

But I didn't know another way to sneak into the alley behind the hardware store without anyone noticing. The sky was still dark, and I didn't want anyone who might be in early to see us slipping past the buildings.

The petal I had seen in the hardware store that dreadful

morning bothered me. I couldn't ask Officer Russell if he had noticed it. I mean, I could, I suppose, but I'm certain he was not happy with me and he clearly wasn't a talker like Pete.

We dropped lower, hidden behind the hardware store. There were no lights in the alley, only a faint sliver from the floodlight in the parking lot of Just Treats. I heard Bean's bell and saw him trample through the fresh snow. Maisie slid off from behind me before I had a chance to properly 'land,' and almost knocked me off in the process.

"Thank God that's over," she muttered under her breath. Pushing her hood off, she brushed the static from her hair with her fingers. "What are we looking for again?"

"*Demittere*," I whispered, grabbing the broom handle before it could fall on the ground. "I saw something in the hardware store." The broom shrunk back into keychain size, and I slipped it into my pocket. "I don't know if the police noticed it, but it seemed out of place." I had never known Eugene to have flowers in his store, and unfortunately, over the last two months, I had visited more times than I could count. The house was slowly falling apart just like the appliances in the café.

"How exactly are we going to get inside?" Maisie walked past me to stand in front of the boards where the rolling service door had once been.

Biting my bottom lip, I stared at all the nails holding the wood board up. I guess I hadn't thought this through very well. We might have to use the front door after all.

I looked down the wall and saw a small window. Standing on my toes, I could barely see inside but it looked like it might be Eugene's office.

"Oh, no." Maisie shook her head. "That window is tiny!"

"Want to go in through the front door?" I asked, crossing my arms.

"No. Someone will notice." She huffed.

"Boost me up." I pointed to the ground.

Maisie threw her head back and sighed. "This is not how I expected my morning to go." She came over to the window and unlocked it with a snap of her fingers. There were moments when I realized just how easy it would be to become a pair of thieves if we wanted to. Thankfully for the residents of Wildewood, I wasn't interested in taking up a life of crime, and yet, here I was about to climb through a window.

With Maisie's help, I wiggled through the small opening, my hips barely making it through. I fell headfirst into the office and laid there, sprawled out, staring up at the dark ceiling. That had not been planned out very well, at all. Groaning, I pushed myself up and stood on my toes to whisper out the window, "Keep a lookout."

"No shit, Sherlock." She grunted.

Sherlock? I giggled. I guess I was . . . Well, a less impressive version. Either way—hello, Wildewood, it's me, Riley Jones, friendly neighborhood witch detective. I doubted anyone would hire me if they knew how I went about figuring things out.

Walking into the main area of the store, I dug a mini flashlight out of my pocket and clicked it on. The beam of light flickered, and I slapped it on the palm of my hand a few times. The flickering subsided. Okay, this needed to be quick. See if the petal was still there, get it, get out. Simple enough, right?

The middle shelf was holding out longer than I had expected. I moved around the store, holding my breath, scared if I breathed too hard it would be the final straw and everything

A Deadly Secret

would topple over. Sweeping the light over the floor, I saw that the blood had mostly been cleaned up but I also saw a faint outline of where it had pooled, staining the cement.

I wanted to believe more than anything that Eugene was alive but . . . I sighed, refusing to finish the thought. Focus, Riley. I could get weepy later when I wasn't breaking and entering. One problem at a time.

Shining the light where I remembered seeing the petal, I heard a noise and almost screeched. The flashlight fell out of my hand and turned off. Lowering into a squat, I held my breath until I saw Bean walk in front of me. Grabbing the flashlight, I clicked it back on. "You scared the shit out of me." I noticed his collar was missing. "Did Maisie send you?" That would explain his missing bell, though even with it, he was stealthy.

The petal stood out like a sore thumb tucked under the foot of the shelf. The police must have deemed it unimportant. Why wouldn't they, though? It was just a flower petal. There were so many other things in this store that could inflict serious bodily harm. Like the dozens of hammers and saw blades scattered around from the scuffle.

I reached for the petal.

Bean hissed, his back arched, and his hair stood.

"It's just a petal," I whispered, slipping it into my pocket. I then bolted back into the office.

Rolling Eugene's chair under the window, I reached for Bean to get him out first. He swatted at me, jumped onto the seat of the chair, then proceeded to jump on the slender window sill. His back paw slipped and I pushed him, which only made him angrier.

Good grief. I had no idea what was up with him, but he

had no interest in me touching or helping him. I was being rejected by both men in my life. Freaking awesome. I mumbled profanities instead of crying like I really wanted to. Standing on the chair, I squirmed to get my shoulders through the small window. This had been much easier the first time.

Maisie grabbed under my arms, pulling as I kicked my feet. As soon as my hips were free, and probably bruised and scraped, I fell into Maisie. We toppled into the snow, me on top.

She pushed me off. "Well, did you get it?"

I brushed snow from my jacket, but it felt weird to the touch. Something wasn't right. My fingertips were tingling, and not in the way they did when I used magic. No—this was painful. I looked back toward the window, wondering what I could've touched that hurt me.

Maisie closed and locked the window with a quick snap. She grabbed my wrist and pulled me down the alley toward the café, the tingling in my fingers fading to a numbness.

Chapter 18

I fumbled with the key to the backdoor. It slipped from my hand into the snow. "*Reserare.*" I snapped my fingers to try unlocking it with magic, but the numbness made it difficult.

Maisie grabbed the keys, giving me a worried look, her brows drawn together and her forehead wrinkled. "What's wrong?" She pushed the door open.

I stared at my fingers. "I don't know."

The overhead lights brightened the kitchen as Maisie turned them on. A shadow blurred across the floor, under the swinging doors, and into the café. I would deal with my numb fingers later. I had been wondering if I'd see the little shadow again, and here it was.

I lost sight of it when I pushed through the swinging doors and walked into the dark café. I held my breath, tip-toeing around the counter, in hopes to catch another glimpse.

Maisie held her hand up, ready to snap her fingers to turn the lights on. I put my hand on top of hers and pushed her arm down. "Wait," I whispered, scanning the room. The only light that came in was from the lamp post outside. I heard movement near the front and thought I heard Bean's bell. That was odd, he hadn't been wearing it. Though, Maisie might've snapped it on him before I fell out of the window.

I opened the door and smacked Zach with it.

Oh my God. "Are you okay?" My jaw dropped. Pulling him inside, his hand cupped his nose, blood dripping toward his lip.

He nodded; his eyes squinted with pain.

"I am so sorry!" I pulled him to the counter and offered him a dry dish rag.

"Good grief, Riley!" Maisie shot me a dirty look as she turned on the fairy lights strung across the ceiling. "I knew you weren't thrilled about hiring another person, but you didn't have to break him." She handed him a damp rag.

I glared at her. "It was an accident."

Zach chuckled, laying the bloodied rag on the counter and picking up the damp one. "I'm okay, really."

"Honest, I thought I heard Bean's bell and"—I waved my hand toward Zach—"I didn't see him standing there."

Zach looked down at his shirt where a few drops of blood had landed. It was barely noticeable on the black fabric. "I'm gonna go clean up in the bathroom." He grabbed the bloodied rags and pushed away from the counter.

As he walked toward the bathrooms, I noticed he was favoring his right leg. Had I hit his leg, too?

"What the hell is going on with you, Riley? You're acting weirder than usual." Maisie crossed her arms.

Me? Acting weird? I huffed at the thought. It was everything else in Wildewood that was weird, not me. Copying her stance, I crossed my arms and turned toward her. "Have you seen anything weird lately?"

"Besides you?" she asked, wiping down the counter where Zach had been.

"I'm serious. Have you?" I saw the shadow again, moving into the hallway. "Like that!" I pointed, skittering after it.

She must've seen it because she was on my heels as I entered the hallway. "What was that?"

Zach stepped out of the bathroom; his nose cleaned up. I looked around but it was too dark to see. Maisie turned the light on, the small bulb lighting up the entire hallway. A little plume of smoke lingered in the corner. I could only assume the shadow I had been following, or that had been following me, had vanished.

"You guys okay?" Zach raised an eyebrow.

My cheeks flushed and I rubbed the back of my neck. "Of course." Why wouldn't I be okay? It wasn't like my fingers were oddly numb and I was definitely not chasing after a shadow creature. Everything is good and normal here. A nervous chuckle came out of me. "Why don't you get the ovens heated." I pulled Maisie into my small office before she had a chance to leave.

"You are seriously acting odd," she whisper-screeched.

Whatever. I waved her statement away with a flap of my hands. "That shadow, whatever it is, found the grimoire for us. We need to figure out how to catch it." I wanted to think it was helping us, but I didn't know. Was it another ghost? Was it something else?

Maisie scowled. "Catch a shadow?"

"Yeah . . ." But how does one catch something that holds

no shape? I rubbed my forehead with the hand that wasn't going numb. If the grimoire wasn't locked, we could probably enlist its help, but until I figured out how to bring the words back to the pages it was useless. "I just don't know how."

I pulled the petal out of my pocket and slipped it into a plastic bag. One problem at a time.

Chapter 19

I scrubbed my hands raw under hot water, hoping to remove whatever had caused the numbness. Everything I touched sent a million hot pinpricks through my fingers. I still hadn't figured out what had caused it. Had there been something on the windowsill? The floor? Or could it have been the flower petal? I knew poisonous plants existed, but I thought they had to be ingested.

I looked around the café. I'd have to set that on the back burner for now. The café was busier than usual with to-go orders. I was hoping we wouldn't run out of paper products before the end of the shift.

Jennifer Mitchell, Ethan's younger sister, strolled into the building. She removed her hat and shook her brown hair out around her shoulders. She smiled when she saw me as she walked to the counter.

"Hey! Are you guys coming by later?" Jennifer worked at Just Treats, the bakery down the street. They were having their re-grand opening in less than an hour.

"We wouldn't miss it." Come to think of it, that was probably why almost everyone in town had come by to get a cup of coffee before the ribbon-cutting ceremony. It was a completely unnecessary thing to do, but the mayor was involved and that usually meant over the top.

"Have you seen my brother?" she asked as I slid a to-go cup her way.

The knife in my heart twisted a bit. "Nope." I handed her a lid.

She fixed her coffee with only one packet of sugar then looked at me with a raised brow. "You guys okay?"

I had no idea, but I didn't want to put any of it on Jennifer's shoulders. "We're fine. He's just been a little . . ." Dismissive? Shut down? "Preoccupied lately." That was a nicer way to say a big hunk of a jerk!

"It's just that time of the month," she mumbled, and it was my turn to give her a look. A laugh bubbled out of her and she swatted at the air. "You know, all men get a little weird occasionally." She secured her lid. "I'll save you a slice of the red velvet cake." She waved and hustled back out.

Scratching my head, I decided to piddle around behind the counter to avoid touching things as much as possible. Maisie and Zach were hovering over the customers who had decided to take a seat and wait. He was picking up the menu rather quickly. Maisie was right, it was nice to have another pair of hands around the café, especially since one of mine wasn't feeling so hot.

The bell chimed, and I looked up to see the mayor walk inside with a long, Burberry vintage checkered coat on, the tie tied tight around her waist, and a lovely scowl plastered on her face. It only deepened when our eyes met, and I wanted to slink away into the kitchen. What could I have possibly done to deserve that? Was she still upset about me sneaking into her vault? I hadn't even been the one to open it! I wasn't even sure any magic known to man could.

"I expect to see you at Just Treats later." She tossed her matching purse on the counter and wiped down the barstool before sitting, even though it was spotless.

"Wouldn't miss it. Would you like a coffee to take with you?" I grabbed a to-go cup since that's what everyone else had requested.

"Your lovely aunt dropped by for a visit this morning." She grabbed a napkin and a wooden stirrer. "It was a good thing I was alone at Town Hall."

I filled her cup with the hot liquid. "What did she want?" Agatha hadn't mentioned anything about making a house call, though let's be honest, Agatha did what she wanted.

"Mostly to just yap my ear off about how I had your family's grimoire. But—" Esther picked up the ceramic cow and poured enough cream to make her coffee almost white. I mooed in my head, wishing I had bought the noisy ones every time she came in. "All she had to do was ask and I would've told her I had it."

"Why *did* you have it?" I questioned.

"Until the two of you showed back up, there wasn't a Wildewood to give it to, and then . . ." She waved her hand in the air dismissively. "I'm a very busy woman, Riley. Things get overlooked. But now you have it."

"I honestly thought it would be bigger," I mumbled. Don't get me wrong, the grimoire was a very large book, but it had been handed down for many generations, and each generation had added to it. There were probably only about five-hundred pages in it. Once unlocked, would we have room to add to it ourselves? Not that I'd have anything to put in there, but Maisie might.

"The grim—" Esther cleared her throat. "The book is bigger than it appears." She stood and slung her purse over her shoulder. "I'll see you at the bakery." She took her coffee and weaved through the crowded café to the exit.

Bigger than it appears? What the hell did that mean? I watched her walk through the café, trying to understand but coming up with a big blank. I would have to ask Agatha about it later. My attention shifted when Pete and John Russell opened the door, waiting for Esther to leave before stepping inside. Pete's cheeks were rosy as he grinned, his eyes flicking toward the display case, and I couldn't help but smile. Don't worry, Pete, we made sure to keep the muffins coming.

I pulled his favorite out and set it on a plate on the counter with a cup of hot water for John Russell with the only tea he had ever asked for. I glanced at Russell and the corner of his lips twitched. Was that a smile? Had I finally won him over? Had he forgiven me for trampling through his crime scene?

"Good morning, officers." I poured Pete a cup of coffee. "Did you ever find Michael?"

"Thanks for the tea." Russell placed a five-dollar bill on the counter. He picked up his tea, a packet of sweetener, then moved to an empty two-seater on the far side of the room.

Okay. I had not won him over just yet. But we were getting there, I could feel it.

"He's not much of a talker." Pete nodded to his partner. "But he's a good cop." He fixed his coffee the way he liked it. "To answer your question, no. Michael hasn't turned up. Has Ethan mentioned if he's seen him or spoken to him?"

I shook my head. "Nope." But right now, Ethan was hiding a lot from me, so who knows.

"Pete." I slipped another muffin onto his plate as he finished half of the first one. There were too many people around to enchant it so that he'd spill any gossip he's heard. Leaning on my elbows, hoping the extra muffin would be enough, I whispered, "I heard the sheriff and Eugene were involved in some business venture together." I dusted the counter. "Do you think that has something to do with his disappearance?"

Pete coughed, patting his chest. His voice was strained as he said, "Wrong pipe." He cleared his throat. "I can't say if it has anything to do with it. But have you ever heard of Peaceful Acres?"

"Yeah, Tessa told me there was a tree farm there. Maisie and I were going to go get one later." It would be nice to have a Christmas tree by Christmas, but we'd see.

"I think the pair were arguing over the land, but I'm not so sure that has anything to do with his disappearance." Pete took a look over his shoulder. Russel was walking back toward us. "Time to go." He winked at me and picked up his unfinished muffin.

Peaceful Acres, huh?

I rubbed my chin, wondering why they'd be arguing over a tree farm. It could be nothing more than a coincidence. They could be investing in the property together . . . although I had never seen Eugene and Manuel interact until this week. There had to be a way to find out more about Peaceful Acres and why it would be worth killing over.

And where Sasha fit into all this.

Chapter 20

Maisie and I stood shoulder to shoulder. Zach stood behind us. And we were all trying not to freeze as we waited for Mayor Esther to finish her speech about how much "the whole town has missed Just Treats." It was true, but it was too damn cold for the lengthy speech. I could feel the cold sinking into my bones, and I just wanted to shove a piece of warm cake into my mouth then maybe snag a cup of the hot cocoa I swear I saw Alice making through the window when we arrived.

"Smile for the camera, dear," Esther said through her teeth as Alice took the pair of ridiculously large scissors and paused for a picture.

The crowd clapped as the red ribbon fell to the ground. Jennifer propped open the bakery doors and we made our way into the building. Thank goodness Just Treats was bigger than the café, but it still didn't leave much room for personal space with the number of people trying to cram their way inside.

I breathed in the decadent smell of fresh cake. My mouth was salivating in anticipation of the red velvet decadence Jennifer promised me. I had missed this smell. It had a tendency to take over this whole side of Wildewood. Almost two months of the renovations from the fire last Halloween had been too long.

The bakery looked the same as it did before the fire. The walls were a comforting sage green and the flooring a light-stained wood. Endless refrigerated display cases housed Alice's cakes and cupcakes for every occasion. Donuts, bagels, croissants, and fresh-baked breads of all kinds. Whatever you wanted, Alice had on these shelves. And if she didn't, she'd make it.

I tucked myself into a corner next to the hot cocoa. Maisie and Zach helped themselves to samples around the store. I poured myself a cup, added a few marshmallows and peppermint flakes, then returned to my spot. Leaning against the window, I closed my eyes, and took a deep breath of the chocolate aroma. Right as I was about to exhale, another scent intruded into my senses and I coughed, spilling the hot liquid onto my hand.

Patchouli.

I grabbed a napkin, looking around to see where the smell had come from, and spotted Jessica Freki walking inside the café. I would never understand why anyone would choose to use that perfume. It was patchouli and . . . something . . . I just couldn't figure out what the other scent was. I wasn't a big fan of patchouli, but that other fragrance was the real problem.

And then a realization washed over me.

I turned around quickly to hide the expression on my face and stared out the window. That smell. That's what was lingering in the hardware store. My heartbeat quickened. I dropped my drink into the trash can, my hands too shaky to hold it. She had been nervous as soon as Pete walked into the café. Was it because she was involved? Had Jessica kidnapped, and possibly murdered, Eugene Fletcher?

"Hey, Riley!"

My heart nearly jumped out of my chest and I spun around. Jessica stood in front of me, dabbing at her nose with a tissue. I plastered a fake smile on my face, but I wanted to get as far away as possible. Was she capable of murder?

How could she have been able to drag someone his size?

She smoothed her curls behind her ears. The skin around her eyes red, as if irritated. I straightened my posture. Play it cool, Riley, everything's okay. There's no way Jessica could have done this. She didn't have the physical strength, not to mention she was currently sick. It was just a coincidence. That's all, just a big, fat coincidence. I shoved my hands in my coat pockets to hide their shaking.

"Hey, Jessica."

She glanced over at Maisie. "Who's the new guy?"

"Zach. We just hired him." I looked past her to see Maisie smile at something Zach said and wished I was standing with them instead of by myself, cornered like a scared animal.

"There's no way those tiny aprons you two wear are going to fit him. Come by the boutique and we'll order some new ones."

Act natural, Riley. "Okay—yeah."

Absolutely no way she could've been involved in Sasha's murder. They were friends. Friends didn't usually murder one another . . . right? That would make for a terrible friend. But she had been angry, and whatever she and Vargas said caused Sasha to run off. Come to think of it, I had no idea where Jessica had gone after that . . .

"Try to come by today." She gave a weak smile before sneezing into her tissue.

While holding the tissue to her nose, she flapped her free

hand in a quick wave before moving away to grab a spot in line. I leaned against the large front window, my heart racing. My fingers gripped the windowsill so hard it turned my knuckles white. I did not want to go to Luna's, but I always ordered custom aprons from her. What if she'd been involved? I closed my eyes and took a deep breath.

Okay—it was possible more people around town were wearing that perfume, though why anyone would was beyond my understanding. It was also possible that the perfume had no connection at all. I needed to focus on the flower petal. I was certain it would lead me to whoever was behind this.

I opened my eyes at the sound of a sneeze. Behind the counter, Jennifer sneezed again. Jessica pulled a tissue out of her pocket and handed it to her. That perfume was so powerful, I'm surprised the whole bakery wasn't sneezing.

I slipped outside, pulling my jacket over my head, and took a seat on an empty wooden bench. A little sad that I didn't get the slice of cake Jennifer had promised me, I stared at the hardware store with the police tape barely hanging on in the wind. It was starting to snow again, thick fluffy snowflakes. A couple of kids running around outside had their mouths open, trying to catch them on their tongues.

The door of the bakery opened, the muted noise from inside grew loud, and Maisie and Zach walked out. "Ready to go?" Maisie stepped in front of me, holding a to-go box. She cracked it open to show me a slice of red velvet cake. "Jennifer told me to give this to you."

Pushing away from the bench, I took the box from Maisie but my appetite hadn't returned. I needed to find out what the connection was with that damn petal. The flowers had already been in the bathroom at Town Hall. If I could find out who delivered the flowers, maybe it would lead me to who killed Sasha and then, hopefully, who took Eugene.

Connie Fields should know. She was Wildewood's florist. The mayor very rarely did her own errands, so someone else had surely picked them up for her and brought them to Town Hall before I got there.

I felt a little better now that I had a plan and secretly wished Maisie had grabbed a fork so I could start eating my cake on the way back to the café. I glanced behind me as we crossed the street and saw Ethan in his blue scrubs walk into the bakery.

My heart sank a little. Maisie must've noticed because she squeezed my hand. I sucked in a deep breath and pushed it aside. There was nothing I could do about Ethan until he was ready to talk to me. Was it too much to ask him to open up, even a little bit? I didn't think so.

I unlocked the café, ready to get out of the cold, but Maisie grabbed my arm and stopped me. She pointed toward the counter where a small gift wrapped in gold paper sat with a red bow on top.

"How did that get there?" I whispered. The café had been locked when we left for the bakery.

"I don't know," she whispered back.

"Do you want me to call the cops?" Zach squeezed by us, walking toward the gift.

I pushed the kitchen doors open, scanning the room for intruders. Maisie walked out of the hallway, shaking her head, and shrugged. Zach turned the gift tag around, and read it aloud, "To my girls." He scrunched his brows and looked at me. "It's not signed."

"Should we open it?" Maisie asked, standing on the other side of me.

I looked between the two of them and wondered what was the worst that could happen. I reached for the bow, and Zach put his hand on my arm. "Are you sure?" I chewed on the inside of my cheek. No, I wasn't sure, but I didn't want to get the cops involved. I had spent too much time with John Russell as it was.

I pulled on the bow and it came loose. Slowly removing the gold wrapping paper, I opened the lid to the brown kraft paper box. Taking out the white tissue paper on top, I reached my hand in and pulled out a heavy, black skeleton key.

"What's that?" Maisie asked.

"I don't know." I palmed the key, trying to understand the intricate design at the top. The teeth at the end looked well-used.

The door chimed and I turned around, holding the key behind my back.

Tessa stood in the doorway; a confused look washed over her face. "What's going on?" She laid her jacket over the closest chair.

I held the key out for her to see and pointed at the empty gift box on the counter. "We have a secret admirer."

Tessa looked at the key and slowly reached out to touch it. She pulled her hand back, but her eyes had already begun dilating. She had a vision. "Oh. That is"—she shook her hand and rubbed it on her jacket—"old."

"The key feels old?" Zach spoke.

Tessa's eyes widened, her hand caught in the cookie jar.

I mentally kicked myself for forgetting, just for a moment, that Zach had no idea what the three of us were. Tessa's nervous laughter bubbled around us and she dismissed him with a wave of her hand. "Yeah, ya know, it's old."

"Don't you own the antique store in town? I would've thought you loved old things."

"Right." She snapped her fingers. "That I do. Hey, you know what that key reminds me of?" She walked behind the counter to help herself to some coffee, which was now probably cold. "Something magical, like what you'd read about in a book."

I raised my brow at her. She was acting weird, not her usual eccentric self. Was she speaking in code? I slipped the key into my coat pocket. "You okay, Tessa?"

She nodded behind her cup of coffee.

"Zach, do you think you could go ahead and get started in the kitchen?" I gave a quick smile and picked up the gift box.

"Sure but—" he started, staring at the box as I threw it in the trash. "I think you should think about beefing up your security. It doesn't seem to be working." He pushed through the swinging doors.

I couldn't argue with him. I picked the box back out of the trash and snatched the tag off the ribbon. The handwriting looked familiar; it was a shame it wasn't signed. Putting the tag into my other pocket, I turned my attention to Tessa.

"That was close." She took a sip of coffee. Her eyes narrowed as she stared off behind me. Setting the cup down, she leaned against the counter, her attention back on me. "Ethan asked if I'd seen you at the grand opening. I got there late, but you probably already knew that. He seemed . . . sad. Trouble in paradise?"

"Ethan's great." He was amazing and made my stomach do weird flippy things when I caught him looking at me. "We just had an argument." A very one-sided argument.

Maisie wrapped an arm around my shoulders, pressing her

cheek against mine. "I'm sure it's nothing. I'm gonna go help Zach get the cupcakes started."

I wish it was nothing, but I was pretty sure it was something. Maisie pushed through the swinging doors, her laughter soon followed. Trying not to feel sorry for myself, I focused on Tessa. "Wanna go with me to Luna's boutique? I need to order new aprons." And I didn't want to go by myself.

"Wish I could but I've gotta get back to the store. Don't worry,"—she patted my hand—"every couple has arguments."

Tessa picked up her jacket, and as she pulled it on, she clicked her tongue and sucked in a long breath. "Don't lose that key. It's important."

"What did you see?" I asked, walking her to the door.

"Nothing specific. Just many different hands using that key. Many, many hands." She gave me a quick hug.

I locked the door behind her, watching her run back to Odds 'n' Ends as a customer was looking into the big front window. I slipped my hand in my pocket, feeling the key. What an odd thing to be gifted. No instructions, no way to know what it was for. What lock even used a key like this anyway? And how did it get inside the café? I'm positive the door had been locked and I had a spell over the café that didn't allow anything in that wished us harm. So, whoever delivered it was a friend. But who?

Chapter 21

With only two hours before the next shift began at The Witches Brew, I made my way around the square, toward Luna's Boutique. My palms were clammy and the dread I was feeling made my legs heavy. The perfume had to be a coincidence. It just had to be.

The door chimed a quick melody as I stepped inside. The scent of patchouli wafted around me, squelching the fresh air from outside immediately. Jessica looked up from her book at the register and a smile spread over her face. She placed her bookmark between the pages and set the book on the glass top.

"Welcome!" She slid off her stool, a tissue going to her nose as she sneezed. Tossing the tissue into a trash can, she walked around the counter. "Still want black aprons?"

I opened my mouth to answer, and she sneezed again, this time into her hands. She looked at her palms and under her breath, excused herself as she made a dash to the bathroom. I looked around the empty store. I rarely came into the boutique. The clothing and jewelry were more high-end than what I wore. Though, maybe I could find something for Maisie while I was here.

Slowly walking down the far-left aisle, I stopped at a wall of jewelry. Everything was new, shiny, and looking at a price tag, out of my price range. It didn't matter, I wasn't sure Maisie would even wear anything from here. We may not have grown up together, but we shared a similar style of dress. Chucks, baggy sweaters, and whatever jeans were comfortable.

I moved to the next aisle, my nose wrinkling as the smell of the perfume grew stronger. In the center of the store on a circular table were a dozen or more perfumes on display. There was a large bouquet in the middle of the table: purple, white, and red flowers, very similar to the ones in the bathroom at Town Hall. I ran the tip of my finger over one of the purple petals, waiting for my finger to go numb as it had before.

Nothing happened.

I picked up a clear perfume bottle and brought it up to my nose. It was a decent fragrance, a little on the fruity side. Placing it back down, a short, round bottle with a long, black atomizer caught my attention. It was pretty, with a chiseled glass design, skewing the view of the deep-purple liquid inside. Spraying it away from me, I sniffed the air and started to cough. I waved my hands in the air in hopes to disperse the smell faster.

This was the perfume I had smelled at the hardware store, and the perfume Sasha had worn, and that Jessica currently wore.

"Isn't it great?" Jessica came up behind me.

I jumped, fumbling the bottle. Regaining my hold on it, I

put the bottle down, suppressing another cough, and nodded. Sure. Yep. Wonderful.

"Here, take a sample." She handed me a small, cylindrical vial. I took it, mostly to not hurt her feelings, and followed her to the register.

I slipped the vial into my pocket. "Is it popular?"

Jessica shook her head, returning to her stool. "No, but I just put it out. It's such an amazing scent." She took in a deep breath, closing her eyes. "There is something about it that I can't quite put my finger on. It's"—she tapped her finger on her chin, her eyes cast to the ceiling—"enchanting, almost."

I'd prefer not to put my finger on it. In fact, I would probably have to change my clothes after I left here. The mist landed all over me instead of on the floor. The whole boutique now reeked of the smell, more so than before. Stifling a chuckle, I imagined Jessica frolicking around the store, spritzing the perfume every few skips. Then I remembered what she might have done and the visual quickly went away.

She laid two black aprons on the counter and pulled a thin, embroidery design book out from under the register. "Want the same thing? Or would you like to try something new?"

"Same design, but . . ." I looked at the two waist aprons. One was longer than the other, the pockets much deeper. "I think we'll go for the longer one this time." I'm sure Zach would appreciate that more than the one he was using.

Jessica pulled out a receipt pad and tallied the price.

"Who all has bought the perfume?" I tried to keep my voice even, hoping I could pry a bit more.

"Just Sasha. I gave her a sample when it first came in."

Her eyes began to water, and I wasn't sure if it was from holding back a sneeze or the memory of her late friend. She handed me the receipt, and then promptly patted at her eyes with a clean tissue. "Perks of being friends with the owner. Well, it was a perk. I'll call as soon as I'm done. Shouldn't take more than a day or two."

"Thanks." I folded the receipt and walked to the door. I started to push it open, stopped, then turned back toward her. "Those flowers you have over there—did you get those from Connie's?"

Her shoulders moved up and down in a shrug. "Sophia brought them in a few days ago. But where else do you get flowers in Wildewood?" Her chuckle was cut short by a sneeze.

I stepped out into the fresh air and tucked my hair behind my ears, going over my list of I don't knows. I didn't know what exactly had transpired between Eugene and Vargas. I assumed it had to do with Peaceful Acres. I didn't know where the flowers came from and if it was even important. I rubbed my temple in a circular motion, trying to make a connection with basically no information.

I pulled the perfume sample out of my pocket, tipping it back and forth, watching the purple liquid move. Only Sasha had received a sample of the perfume, because, well, it stunk. But she was dead, so she couldn't have killed or kidnapped Eugene. Jessica sure as hell loved the perfume, and she's the only other person I had smelled it on. But was the perfume even important? What motive did Jessica have to hurt her best friend and Eugene?

Maybe she wasn't working alone . . .

I looked out into the street, scanning the snow-covered square. It was too cold to hang out on the lawn, though a few kids were throwing around misshapen snowballs. Their laughter brought a smile to my lips. A rogue snowball flew toward Town Hall, hitting the back end of a police cruiser. Could the sheriff be involved? I placed the sample back in my pocket and decided to make one last stop before I went back to the café.

Chapter 22

I poked around outside of Connie's Flowers, searching the wide vases for purple flowers. Most of what was on the cart outside were red carnations, roses, and white gardenias. Nothing like what I had seen in the bathroom at Town Hall. The doors slid open when I stepped in front of them.

It was almost as cold inside as it was outside. I pulled my jacket tighter around my waist and swore I could see my breath. There was a full wall lined with display refrigerators with flowers of all colors stuffed in their vases. Boxes of premade corsages and boutonnieres. There were flowers around the store I knew weren't in season, such as the row of tulips in every color imaginable. There was even a tall floor vase filled with sunflowers.

I didn't know how she did it, but Connie always had off-season flowers.

The middle of the store was set up with premade arrangements in different sized vases. I walked to them, trying to find the one from Luna's boutique and Town Hall. None of them looked right. There were bouquets that were purple and white.

Red and purple. Even a few that were red and white. But none with all three colors together.

Looking over at the counter, Connie still hadn't appeared. She must be in the back; I could hear movement: the shuffling of feet and what sounded like loud pops that I hoped was her cutting stems.

On the wall opposite the refrigerators, flowers were color-coded. I approached the containers of purple flowers, trying to find any with similar petals. A curved petal, the tip folded toward the middle, kind of resembling a hood. It wasn't a small petal, not like one from an aster. The petal of the pansy was spread open.

I ran my finger down the petal of a wisteria flower. It wasn't as deep of a purple, but the shape was as close as I could find. My finger didn't tingle, didn't go numb. It wasn't that one. Maybe Sophia hadn't gotten the flowers from Connie's after all. Or Jessica just told me that to throw me off her trail.

Connie popped out of the backroom. Her straight, silver hair was cut in a layered bob. She had a bright-green apron tied around her slender waist that read "Connie's Flowers" with little sunflowers embroidered on it. She set a short, round vase on the counter filled with the combination of flowers I had been looking for.

"Riley! What a surprise!" She pushed her black, coke-bottle glasses up her nose. "Have you decided The Witches Brew could use some flowers?" She grinned, giving me a wink.

"Actually . . . I was looking for this arrangement." I turned the vase, inspecting the flowers.

"Well, you're in luck. It's the last one." Her grin widened.

"Is this the same one from Luna's and Town Hall?" It looked identical but I wasn't an expert on flowers.

Connie rubbed her chin, tilting her head, and gazed at the ceiling. "I think so. Let me check."

She grabbed a large invoice binder out from behind the counter. It made a loud thud as she dropped it. Opening the cover, she turned quickly to a page labeled "December." She ran her finger down the list, and I was surprised at just how long it was. Her finger finally stopped, and she moved her glasses down to the tip of her nose.

"Yes. This is the exact arrangement." She leaned a bit closer to the page. "Oh, dear."

"What's wrong?" I stood on my toes, trying to see what she was seeing. Her handwriting was messy, and I couldn't make out anything.

"It looks like I can't sell this one to you after all. The mayor ordered a replacement." She looked up, her eyes going from one side of the shop to the other. "Where is Daisy?"

"The daisies are—" I started to point, my hand falling short. She meant her employee. She had two girls working for her. Word around the rumor mill said they were her granddaughters but she would never confirm or deny it. "She wasn't here when I came inside."

Connie rolled her eyes and sighed.

"Would you like me to take it to the mayor? I really don't mind."

"That girl is driving me up the wall. She's always missing. I'm surprised she got the first one delivered on time." Connie huffed. She walked to the edge of the counter and pulled on a red ribbon. Cutting it at the length she wanted, she walked back to the vase and tied a neat bow. "I would greatly appreciate it."

"It's my pleasure." I took the vase, holding it away from my body just in case. "Could you do me a favor though?"

"Anything. You're saving me from an earful from Esther." Connie chortled.

"Would you call Maisie for me at the café, and let her know I'll be a little late."

"Consider it done." Connie thanked me as I walked out of the flower shop.

I touched one of the petals, and again, nothing happened. At this point, I was starting to think the original arrangement had been tampered with. Was it possible that Daisy had added, or switched out flowers in the bathroom at Town Hall? The way my fingers went numb after touching the petal from the hardware store made me believe it had been used to subdue Eugene. Could the same have happened to Sasha?

I wish I knew what it was. I could've asked Connie, but I wasn't sure I could trust her. I liked Connie, but I didn't 'know' Connie.

I walked into Town Hall and saw Esther disappear into her office. She poked her head out of the doorway, her eyes narrowed at me. "What are you doing here?"

Resisting the urge to roll my eyes, I held out the flower arrangement. "Connie asked me to bring these to you."

"What happened to what's her name?" Esther took the vase.

"Daisy? I don't know." I followed her to the receptionist's desk where she gently set the vase down. "Do you remember if she was the one who brought the flowers here before the Christmas party?"

Esther shrugged her shoulders, messing with the flowers to change how Connie had arranged them. "I couldn't tell you."

Her hands stilled, and she looked at me. "Why? What are you getting yourself into?"

She could see right through my questions. My cheeks heated, and I bit my bottom lip. "No reason." I said a quick goodbye then made a B-line for the door. The sound of Esther's heels chased after me, and her hand slapped the door before I had a chance to open it. Damn, she was fast when she wanted to be.

"Stay out of it, Riley." And that was all she said. She turned around and walked back to her flowers.

I stood in the doorway for a second, my mouth hanging open as I decided if I should question her statement. Did she know what was going on? She had certainly caught on quick.

"Goodbye, Riley," Esther said, making my decision for me.

Pulling my hood over my head, I jogged across the street toward the square. What the hell was going on in this town? Did everyone know something I didn't? To be honest, I wasn't surprised by Esther. She knew everything. Well, almost everything. But did she know who killed Sasha? Was she protecting someone?

Chapter 23

Pete yawned as he walked into the café. He shuffled to the barstool he always sat on. I really should just write "reserved for Pete" on it. Blinking his eyes slowly, he yawned again. I poured a cup of decaf for him. It was late, he had just gotten off his shift. It was a new change in his café routine.

Pete accepted it and looked into the cup before glancing up at me. "John thinks I should start drinking chamomile tea after work." He poured sugar into the cup. "But I told him I had already switched to decaf and he can shove his chamomile you know where." He chuckled.

"You did not." I smiled, knowing Pete would never say anything like that.

"No, but I thought it." He took a sip, grimacing behind the rim.

I chuckled. Should I tell him it all tastes the same? I probably shouldn't, otherwise, he might tell me to shove my decaf "you know where." Instead, I asked, "How's the sheriff doing?"

It was almost closing time. Maisie and Zach were in the kitchen doing dishes. There were a few stragglers sitting around the dining room and a couple of teenagers lounging together on the plush, black couch. The evening shift had gone by quickly, which wasn't surprising with how busy we had stayed. I was definitely not regretting hiring Zach. He was picking up the menu quicker than I expected.

"He's a mess. But who wouldn't be after finding out how his wife passed?" Pete sighed into his cup.

Tapping my finger to my lips, I tried not to seem too interested, but couldn't pass up the opportunity. "I can't imagine how he's feeling. How did she . . ."

"The medical examiner called this afternoon, ya know, the one from Twin Falls." We didn't have our own medical examiner, so of course, our neighbor, Twin Falls, did. Pete leaned closer to me. "She suspects poison."

Poison? That would explain the lack of blood at the scene. Though it didn't explain why Sheriff Vargas had immediately assumed murder.

"Wow." My movements slowed. I didn't know what to say to him that wouldn't give up certain 'illegal' things I'd been up to recently.

"She found a flower petal in Sasha's throat. Can you believe that? A flower!" Pete's voice echoed through the room, and the couple on the couch shifted to look at him.

I motioned for him to lower his voice, but now I knew the petal I had found really was important. It was the key to finding out who killed Sasha and, presumably, Eugene. If she had been poisoned by a plant, Eugene was probably not with us anymore. My stomach knotted and I took in a deep breath, trying to keep the tears from my eyes.

"That's terrible," my voice broke, betraying the cool demeanor I tried to portray.

"Sure is." Pete stood, taking the last sip of his coffee. He made another face as if the coffee truly tasted differently. "Thanks for the nightcap." He slid me a few dollars.

After the last customer paid, I retreated into my office and opened the top drawer of my desk. The petal, still in the plastic bag, laid on top of all the other junk I kept in the drawer. Dropping into my chair, I stared at it, wondering what plant it could be from and how it had come to Wildewood.

I needed to go to the library—I didn't own a computer, not even a cell phone. Since I came into my powers, electronics had a tendency to get zapped when I touched them. It was something I missed from my days before Wildewood, but not something I was willing to trade back.

I checked my watch. Damn, the library had just closed. I would leave early tomorrow, and hopefully, I'd get to the bottom of it. I tapped a finger to my chin. I should probably bring someone with me who could help me use the computer. Tessa might be willing, but she also might tell me to stay out of it. I grabbed the plastic bag, shoving it into my pocket, and pushed the drawer shut.

"See you tomorrow." Maisie pulled the front door closed after Zach walked through. She folded his apron, a smile touching her lips, as she turned away from the door. She looked up at me, trying to hide her smile, but the creases around her eyes gave her away.

"Ready?" I grabbed my jacket and bag, double-checking to make sure the skeleton key was in the small, zippered pocket in the back. I was ready to go home. I had so much on my mind from the gift of our secret admirer, learning that Sasha had been poisoned to Ethan and his secrets. It was truly exhausting.

Chapter 24

Snow tracked onto the hardwood as we scrambled to get in from the cold. The look Maisie had given me when I asked if she wanted to 'ride' home could've killed me. I pulled my jacket off, more snow falling onto the ground, and hung my bag up. Maisie made a brisk walk to the kitchen, grabbing two packets of hot cocoa.

I headed for the stairs, stopping when I heard a whisper. Slowly turning, I walked back down the steps, my socked feet slipping when I got to the bottom. I grabbed onto the railing to pull myself back up. The whispering continued, and I followed the voice toward the back of the house.

Agatha walked through the back door, and I yelped. "Good grief!"

"What's wrong?" Maisie came running into the hallway.

"I think we need to put a bell around your neck." I flicked my eyes to the ceiling. I could not count how many times she'd popped up out of the blue and almost given me a heart attack.

"You wouldn't dare." She glared at me.

I might, Auntie. I just might. But instead of provoking her further, I walked around her—though I probably could've walked through her—and opened the back door. Sticking my head out, I looked back and forth on the porch. "Who were you talking to?"

"No one." She crossed her arms.

There were little paw prints from the steps to the railing and then back down the steps. Bean had been here. I started to wonder if he was avoiding us for some reason. I shut the door and mimicked her posture.

The microwave beeped. Maisie walked back into the kitchen. A moment later, she yelled, "Cocoa's ready."

I walked past Agatha but could feel her hovering on my heels. I went to my bag and took out the key.

"We got a present today." I turned toward her and held the key in the air.

Agatha's lips parted, her eyes widened. She reached for the key. Her body flickered and she dropped her hand back to her side. "Go get the grimoire."

I laid the key on the counter then ran up the steps to my dresser. Before heading back down, I pulled my socks off. The last thing I needed was to fall down the steps and break something. I laid the book on the island, still wrapped in the brown paper. Agatha swiped her hand in the air above the book. The corner of the paper peeled, ripping down the middle to expose a keyhole.

"Who gave this to you?" Agatha asked, motioning to the key. It rose into the air, floating toward the grimoire.

"We don't know," I answered. I had thought maybe Agatha had left it, but I doubt she was the type to wrap a gift with a neat bow on top. Now that I thought about it, she had no reason to leave it at the café when she lived in my house. Maybe the shadow had . . .

"It was signed 'to my girls,'" Maisie added as she placed a steaming cup of chocolate in front of me.

I brought it to my nose, taking a deep inhale of the creamy chocolate aroma, wishing we had some peppermint candies. I was a little sad that I didn't get to partake in the peppermint hot cocoa at Just Treats.

The key fell to the counter and Agatha huffed. "Would one of you—" She flapped her hand around. "I just don't have it in me tonight."

I placed the warm mug down then picked up the key. It was long and brittle-feeling, though that could just be the exterior paint. Looking at the intricate design at the top of the key, I realized it was a pair of Ws.

Wildewood.

There was no strap that fit under the keyhole. Nothing to 'lock' the book closed, but I proceeded to insert the key into the cover. Twisting it, I removed the key and the book opened. A table of contents appeared, written in many different scrawls. I flipped the pages, the table of contents longer than any I had ever seen, and in no particular order. It would take hours to find anything.

I glanced at Agatha. Her eyes glistened. She put her hand over the book, barely touching it. "I have been searching for that key."

"When you said the key to the grimoire, I didn't realize you meant an actual key," I admitted.

"It's to keep it safe from non-Wildewoods."

I flipped to the middle of the book. "How do we find anything in here?"

"You think it," she answered curtly. "Go on. Give it a try. Hold your hands over the pages."

I placed my palms above the book and thought about the shadow—I didn't know what else to call it. I was pretty sure it wasn't a ghost, but beyond that, I had no clue. I knew it was small and sneaky. It was fast and seemed timid. The pages began to flip, fanning my hands, and then it stopped abruptly.

Ink appeared as if it were being written now and not many years ago. My fingers trailed down the page, the ink was dry. That was a neat trick. At the top of the page, in an immaculate script, "Hobgoblins." There was a small paragraph explaining what a hobgoblin was, but the cliff notes version was: A sneaky creature, easily scared, and often up to no good, but very loyal to its owner.

"What exactly were you thinking?" Agatha asked.

"I've been seeing this little shadow . . . I think it's what left the key for us."

She *hmmed* in response.

Taking in the bits of information down the page, I noticed someone had scribbled a note near the bottom about how to catch a hobgoblin. Perfect, I thought and pulled a notebook out of the junk drawer next to the sink.

Agatha was looking over my shoulder, and I clicked the pen. "Does this mean something to you?" I asked her.

"Not sure." Her eyes seemed distant. "I'll be back."

Agatha snapped her fingers and vanished in a cloud of smoke, leaving Maisie and me alone to fan it away. Of course, she'd poof away, like always, instead of telling us what was going on. Maisie picked up her cup and came to stand next to me. We paged through the book for a while, stopping occasionally to look over spells.

Tears stung the corner of my eyes. I was in awe. It felt amazing to hold a compilation of all the Wildewoods since their beginning. Every spell they used, and the occasional recipe. We literally had our entire family history stored in one, very large, book.

I finally closed it; my eyes tired from trying to read the script.

Maisie took the book into her room to continue to look through it. I climbed up the stairs, kicking my shoes off. My pinky toes ached from the new boots. I missed the ones I had thrown out. After changing into a mismatched set of pajamas, I laid on my stomach on my bed with the perfume sample and the flower petal in front of me.

I picked up the sample and unscrewed the little plastic top. Sniffing, I gagged and held it away. I suppose everyone had their own likes in perfume but I just couldn't get over this one. I took another sniff. Jessica was right though, there was something else in it that I, also, couldn't put my finger on. I blinked, my eyes watering and my nose numb. I wiggled my nose, wondering if there was something in the grimoire that could help.

I was positive the flower petal was the key to finding out who killed Sasha and, probably, Eugene, but what I still didn't understand was where Peaceful Acres fit into the puzzle. Eugene and Vargas were arguing over the land—but who owned it? Were they trying to buy it together or was it a disagreement over money?

If this issue was between Eugene and Vargas, why did Sasha end up dead?

I rolled off the bed to lay the items on the dresser and saw Natalie Remington's business card. Holding it between two fingers, I decided I would pay her a visit. Wildewood Realty was the only real estate group in town. Surely, someone could tell me who owned Peaceful Acres and shed some light on the situation.

Chapter 25

I woke up in a crabby mood and brushed it off to having not spoken to Ethan. I would be lying if I said I didn't miss him. I did. I missed his smile, his deep-set dimples, and the way his eyes lit up when he looked at me. Ignoring the hurt I was feeling as much as I could, I dragged myself out of bed. Maybe I was being too stubborn waiting for him to come to me, but I couldn't be with someone who brushed off anything and everything deep.

After getting ready, I noticed the answering machine was blinking and secretly hoped it had been a message from Ethan—I rarely checked it, only when I was expecting a call—instead, it was an old message from Eugene letting me know he would be delivering the oven in the morning. Of course, this was from a few mornings ago. Hearing his voice brought tears to my eyes because I knew we may never see him again.

I shoved the perfume sample, the petal, and Natalie's business card into my bag before heading out. The sidewalks were buried under a few inches of snow that had fallen overnight. Maisie shivered next to me as we walked up the street to the café, mumbling about needing to get a car.

A car would definitely come in handy during the winter and the hottest part of summer. And days it rained. I guess I could retire my broom. Scratch that—I would not be retiring my broom any time soon. Unlike Maisie, I enjoyed flying above the trees, as long as it listened to me.

We got to work on our morning duties. I slid a tray into the new oven, feeling thankful for its quick installation, but a knot formed in the pit of my stomach as I set the time. This had been the last thing Eugene had done for me, and I hadn't had a chance to keep my promise: A dozen muffins of his choosing. I didn't even know which one he favored.

I hoped I had the opportunity to ask him. I would never forget.

After the first rush of eager customers, I grabbed the phone off the cradle and went to hide in my office. Maisie and I planned on setting our 'trap' for the shadow—er, I mean, hobgoblin—this evening. But we needed a silver cage. The grimoire hadn't been very specific as to why, just that there was something about pure silver that caused the little creature to not sense magic. Or maybe it was the cage itself it couldn't sense? I didn't care either way, as long as it worked.

I called Tessa to see if she had a critter cage made of silver but it appeared she drew the line at animal things, and it shocked me. I honestly thought Tessa took in everything, not realizing she had lines drawn. Feeling unsuccessful, I placed the phone back behind the counter and thought of who else I could call.

I looked up at the sound of the door chime to see Esther walking inside.

Perfect.

I poured a to-go cup for her as she found her way to the counter.

"Good morning, Madam Mayor." I set the cup in front of her and laid out a napkin with a spoon. "Would you like a muffin or a scone this morning?"

Esther's nose wrinkled as she glanced into the display case. "I'll pass." She slid the cup closer and picked up the small, ceramic cow to add cream into her coffee. "Have you figured out how to use the book?" She glanced up at me, her eyes squinting, and I stopped mooing in my head.

I studied her as she stirred sugar into her coffee. Should I tell her we had been gifted the key to the grimoire? I wasn't sure how she would react; I didn't think she wanted us to have it to begin with. "Not yet." Damn, I was becoming quite the little liar. "I have a question . . ." She laid the spoon down on the napkin and tasted the coffee. I wasn't sure if she was tuning me out or not, but I continued, "I was wondering if you had a particular item I could borrow."

Esther ripped the top off another packet of sugar. "What item might that be?"

She had a very strange way of showing she was listening. "A silver cage." I took the trash from the counter and threw it away.

Snapping the lid on her to-go cup, Esther wiped at a small droplet on the side. "Why exactly do you need a silver cage?"

Glancing around the café, I didn't want anyone to overhear us, I lowered my head and whispered, "I'm trying to catch something that's been following us."

"Hmm." She stood. "Having critter problems? I'm surprised that cat of yours can't take care of it. Though, he has always been a little lazy." She looked around the café before her eyes met mine. "I'm on my way to Town Hall. Why don't you walk with me?"

I removed my apron and ran to the far-right corner of the café to tell Maisie I'd be right back. With my jacket in my arms, I held the door for Esther and we began our short walk across the snowy square to Town Hall.

"I take it you found the key." Esther placed her hood over her perfectly-pinned-back hair.

My cheeks heated. I lowered my eyes to the ground. "We did." She was as sharp as a tac. I didn't know why I even bothered keeping anything from her.

"Hmm."

Our shoes crunched on the patches of ice covering the walkway. Esther wore heels and I was in awe at how she could be so poised, never slipping on the slick pathway. I was in boots and I could feel my feet about to give out with each step. Did she enchant her shoes? Is that why she never wobbled? I would be needing that spell pronto.

"Have you figured out how to navigate through the grimoire? It's much bigger than it seems." That wasn't the first time she had said that.

"Sort of. I was able to find a page on how to trap my . . . shadow." My foot slipped as we stepped onto the street.

"A shadow?"

I held my arms out as I teetered, trying to catch my balance. "That's all I can see. A little shadow moving around and then it disappears," I admitted, leaving out that the book called it a Hobgoblin. She didn't need to know what it was.

"Interesting." Esther led me down to the vault. She held her hand up. The handle began to spin. Clicking sounds came from the large door, echoing in the stairwell. It creaked open and I followed Esther as she stepped inside.

She stopped at a shelf near the back of the room and moved a tall stool forward to stand on. Climbing up three steps, Esther pulled a white sheet off an item at the very top and dropped it to the floor, exposing a small silver birdcage. She didn't slip once as she climbed back down and I knew, I just knew, she had to be using some type of magic. She set the cage on one of the tables in the middle of the room. I looked around as I made my way to it. She had so many items. More than I remembered the first time I came into this room. My eye caught a row of necklaces, large pointed stones attached to silver chains. I had never seen a necklace like it, let alone a half dozen of them.

"Pendulums." She nodded toward the jewelry. "Witches use them to scribe for things."

Pendulum? Scribe? I had no idea what she was talking about. Agatha was right. I might be a twenty-eight-year-old woman, but my magic was at a kindergarten level. Actually, it was probably worse.

"Certain creatures cannot feel magic within the cage. If your shadow is what I think it is, this will do the trick." Esther tapped her finger on the door and symbols etched into the frame glowed. "There." She handed it to me.

"What do you think the shadow is?"

"Your family had many creatures that served their needs." She handed me the white sheet to cover the cage back up. "I imagine some of those creatures might be looking for you. I'm sure word of yours and Maisie's return to Wildewood has gotten around to things that have been waiting."

A shiver went down my spine. Things were waiting for our

141

return? I wondered if we should be more concerned about the little creature following me around. It seemed harmless, but perhaps it was a good thing we were one step closer to figuring out exactly what it was and what it wanted.

I thanked her, taking the cage and her cryptic message with me back to the café.

Chapter 26

The sun had set. More snow had fallen in the past few hours. The temperature outside was cold enough that the snow stuck. Even though the café was warm, each time the door opened, it dropped a few degrees. I contemplated talking Maisie into another broomstick ride, so we didn't have to be in the cold for long. I watched her smile at Zach as he took the stack of dishes out of her hands. It was good to see her happy. On second thought, I wouldn't ask her. She would probably hit me with the broom if I even hinted at it.

Maisie turned her head and caught me staring. My eyes widened. She weaved through the café and laid the dishes on the counter. "You're being creepy."

I scoffed. "Am not!"

The corners of her lips curled, and she glanced behind her. "I feel like I've known him for a while. Is that how you felt with Ethan?" My smile faltered and she grimaced. "Oh, I'm sorry. You guys still haven't talked?"

"It's fine." I picked up the dishes. "Maybe we aren't meant to be." My voice trailed off at the sound of the door chime.

Ethan stepped into the café. He brushed the snow off the shoulders of his jacket then ruffled his hair before glancing up. The ice surrounding my heart began to melt. My chest tightened. I took a shaky breath. I hadn't expected to see him. Not yet.

"Excuse me," I whispered to Maisie then ducked into the kitchen. The doors swung wildly behind me, and I placed the dishes in the sink a little more aggressively than I meant to.

Grabbing the sides of the basin, I closed my eyes and took in a deep breath, trying to slow the accelerated beating of my heart. Did I want to talk to him? Yes. Was I going to? Probably not. God, why was this so hard? I wanted to run into his arms and kiss his soft lips. But I also wanted him to stop hiding stuff from me.

"Riley?"

My eyes popped open; my body tensed. I could see Ethan's distorted reflection in the chrome fixtures of the sink as he stood behind me. "Are you avoiding me?"

Me? Ha! I exhaled sharply through my nose. Spinning around, I placed my hands on my hips. "Why would I be avoiding you? It wasn't as if you wham-bam-thank-you-ma'amed me. It's totally acceptable to sleep with someone and then kick them out right after." I poked my finger into his chest. His perfectly chiseled chest. "Just because you avoid deep conversations doesn't give you the right to—"

He pressed my hand against his chest. I could feel his heart beating as quickly as my own.

"You're right. I'm sorry." His eyes softened.

I blinked, speechless. I had not expected an apology. His baby blues twinkled, and I could feel their pull. "Apology mostly accepted."

"Mostly?" He smirked, a dimple forming in his right cheek and that was all it took for me to become a weak pile of sap on the floor. Curse you, dimples! Ethan wrapped his long fingers around my hand. "What can I do to get you to fully accept my apology?" He brought my knuckles to his mouth and gently kissed them. Curse those incredibly supple lips too.

I could feel his hypnotic stare take hold. Remember, Riley, he was a jerk. A big, beautiful jerk, but a jerk nonetheless. I closed my eyes to resist his lure. "You can start by letting me in a little." Taking my hand back, I crossed my arms and noticed he was holding a manila envelope under his arm. "What's that?"

He handed it to me. "The picture you asked me to enlarge."

I had forgotten, with everything going on. I pulled out the picture, hoping he had been able to capture what I'd seen. It was dark and hard to see any details.

"I told you there wasn't anything there besides a shadow," Ethan said.

Squinting, I brought it close to my face. He was wrong. There was a shape within the shadow. I walked past him into the café. Zach was telling the last customer bye as he held the door for them. Maisie was behind the counter, and I handed her the picture. "Do you see anything?"

She squinted at it. "What am I supposed to be looking at?"

"Look at the shadow . . . for . . . another shadow."

"A shadow in a shadow?" Ethan took the picture and held it close to his nose. "Riley, I don't see anything." He handed it back to Maisie, unconvinced.

"There is something there. Hold on." I ran around the counter and into my office. Rummaging around in the bottom drawer full of random things, I found a magnifying glass. I ran back behind the counter and held it over the right corner of the picture. "There's a shape."

Maisie leaned over my arm; her nose close enough to create a fog on the magnifying glass. "It's a . . ."

"A shadow." I finished her thought. "*The* shadow."

If it really was the same thing—the hobgoblin—I had been seeing, it's been around for a while. I glanced behind me at Zach. He turned the open sign to closed and began wiping down a table.

"I don't see it." Ethan shrugged. "But whatever it is, I'm glad I could help."

I slid the picture back into the manila folder. "I could use your help with one more thing, if you don't mind."

"Does this mean you forgive me completely?" His warm hand found mine.

Maisie excused herself to go help Zach. I tugged Ethan close to me, tilting my head back to look into his eyes. He wrapped an arm around my waist, pressing us tightly together. His vanilla scent flooded my senses. Stay strong, Riley, but my knees already felt weak and I was glad he was holding me up.

"Mostly. Would you mind going to the library with me? It's going to close soon but I need someone's help with the computer."

He rubbed his chin with his free hand. "You need help with the computer?"

Ah—surely he noticed I didn't have a cell phone. "Electronics and I don't get along. It won't take long, I promise." I hoped because the library was about to close.

Chapter 27

The library was warm; half of the fluorescent lights above were turned off, creating a cozy atmosphere. I could hear a few hushed conversations, but otherwise, the library was empty. I pulled my jacket off before we reached the circulation desk. The woman who usually set behind it was missing. The squeak of a wheel echoed and then I saw her pushing a cart filled with books toward the back of the building.

She looked up and placed her glasses on her nose from a strap hanging around her neck. "We're closing in twenty. Need any help?"

I waved at her. "No, we'll be very quick."

Pulling Ethan toward the far-right wall, I pushed him into a hard-plastic chair in front of a computer screen. His knees bent awkwardly, the desk not designed for someone of his stature. He signed in using my library card and we waited, watching the loading symbol spin while the computer logged in.

"What are you looking for?"

I pulled the neighboring chair close to his, my knees touching his leg. "I need you to look up books on poisonous plants."

147

Ethan glanced at me before putting his fingers to the keyboard. "Why do you need a book on poisonous plants?"

"It's best you don't know." I placed my hand on his thigh.

Ethan pulled up the catalog and typed in the search bar. A surprisingly long list of books appeared, but most weren't located in the library at Wildewood. I didn't have time to wait for a book to come in, I needed one tonight. He changed the search perimeters and a single book was left.

"That's a little disappointing," I mumbled. Careful not to touch the computer, I grabbed a short, yellow pencil, and on a small square of paper scribbled down the call number.

"Is that it?" Ethan moved the mouse to the X on the browser.

"Hopefully."

He signed out of the computer and then we headed to the agricultural section. Ethan walked behind me, and out of the corner of my eye, I saw a dark shape move within his shadow. I stopped. Ethan bumped into me, gripping my upper arms. I wiggled free and followed the shadow as it moved against the bottom of the bookshelves.

Reaching the end of the bookcase, I lost sight of it. Frustration fluttered inside me and I looked up to see the sign for "Agricultural." We walked into the aisle and a book on the second-highest shelf moved. It wobbled out from between its neighboring books and fell to the carpeted floor in a muted thud.

"What the hell . . ." Ethan stepped in front of me and picked up the book. He looked into the gap it had come from, then looked at me. "What was that?"

"The shadow." I took the book from his hand.

"Looks like you didn't need my help after all." He laced his fingers in mine as we walked to the circulation desk.

The woman had returned, her cart empty. I handed her the book and my library card. Her lips moved; eyes focused on the title. "That's funny." She scanned the book, the corners of her eyes crinkled as she laughed. "For such an odd book, you're the second person this month to check it out."

Second person?

My stomach twisted. I gave her a chuckle, though I didn't see the humor. I licked my dry lips and asked, "Who was the first person?"

She stared at her screen. "Hmm . . ." Her brows scrunched. "Oh, that's weird."

"What?" I leaned over the desk, trying to see what she was looking at.

"So sad. It says Sasha Vargas checked it out." She handed me the book.

I winced, recovering as quickly as I could to hide how I felt. Sasha had checked out a book about poisonous plants and then ended up dead, with a petal from one shoved down her throat. I placed the book in my bag, told her goodbye, and forced myself to walk, not run, out of the library.

Ethan grabbed my arm and turned me to face him. "What's going on?"

I avoided eye contact. It would be wrong of me to lie to him, to hide things from him, since I had been so upset with him doing that to me. But what if I put him at risk by telling him all that I knew? Which was still not much, but enough.

"Did you drive to work?" I looked around. There were still people out and about, not many, but more ears than I wanted.

"Yeah, I parked behind Just Treats."

I took his hand. "Come on. I'll tell you in the truck."

Chapter 28

Ethan didn't say much as we sat in his truck in the overflow parking lot behind the bakery. Only one working lamp chased away the darkness, casting an eerie yellow glow. The moon was almost full, resting high above the trees. Snow fluttered onto the hood of the truck and quickly melted away.

I told him about the petal I saw at the hardware store. I left out the part where I committed a felony in order to retrieve it. Then I told him about the petal found in Sasha's throat. He only made a few noises in response.

"I think Eugene is in trouble." Assuming he wasn't already dead. I pulled the book out of my bag, running my hand over the hardcover.

Ethan straightened his posture and stared out the window. His brows were drawn together, his lips thin. His nostrils flared and he wrapped his hands around the steering wheel. I watched him let out a breath, his voice quiet. "I think so, too."

He pulled out of the parking lot, turning on to the main road that led out of the center of town. I glanced at him, noting how tight his jaw seemed. Looking back to my lap, I flipped the book to the table of contents. Since I didn't know what I was looking for, it wasn't helpful. Neither was the glossary. I would have to look at each picture and hope to find a match.

We rode in silence until he parked the truck in front of my house. I didn't take it personally. I had dumped a lot of information in his lap and he needed to digest it.

I slid the book back into my bag and turned to face him, placing my hand on his, which still gripped the steering wheel. His face softened, his hand taking mine. "Would you be willing to let me borrow your truck tomorrow evening? We still haven't gotten a Christmas tree."

He leaned across the bench seat and kissed me before I had a chance to react. My breath caught in my throat, and only when he pulled away could I breathe again. "Where are you getting one from?"

"Tessa told me Peaceful Acres has a tree farm."

His Adam's apple bobbed and he licked his lips. "Are you sure you want a real tree? They can be a pain."

And a fake tree wasn't? I cocked my head and raised an eyebrow. Either he didn't want me to borrow his truck or he didn't want me to go to Peaceful Acres. "I'm sure we can strap it to the top of Tessa's car. It's okay." I was positive I could not tie one to my broom.

Ethan ran his hand over the back of my head until it rested on the base of my neck. "No, it's fine. But how about I pick you guys up? I'll even chop it down for you."

I gave him a smile, trying to keep the skepticism off my face. "That sounds wonderful. I'm closing the café after the morning shift. Want to pick us up here before it gets dark?"

He nodded, bringing my knuckles to his lips. I slid closer,

running my hand through his hair, and pressed my lips to his. It had only been a short while, but I missed the feel of his lips. Though, his kiss seemed stiff this time. Pulling away, I got out of the truck, readjusted my bag on my shoulder, and waved as he turned around in the driveway.

I waited until I could no longer see his taillights. He tried to hide how he was feeling, but I suspected he knew more about Eugene's disappearance than he was admitting. He was, after all, friends with Michael, and I bet Michael had confided in him.

I walked inside and saw the silver cage sitting on the kitchen island. Maisie sat next to it, her feet swinging as she scooped a spoonful of cereal into her mouth.

"Everything good?"

"I think so." I hoped so.

"Ready to catch a shadow?" She placed the bowl beside her and scooted off the counter to stand on her fuzzy, black slippers. Her long hair was wet and she wore a matching set of red, plaid pajamas.

She handed me the grimoire and grabbed the handle at the top of the cage. Following me behind the stairs, I laid the book on the floor and held my hands over it just as I had before. The pages flipped, opening back to the page for hobgoblins.

What a peculiar name for a creature.

I placed the cage in the corner. Maisie set a small, chrome bowl with cream in as far back as she could inside the cage.

"Are you sure this is going to work?" She sat back on her haunches beside me.

Nodding, I ran my finger over the instructions, rereading them quickly.

"Do we have to recite a spell or anything?"

"It doesn't say." I picked the book up and stood. "The cream will lure it in and then—" I slammed the door closed. Maisie jumped, bumping her head on the stairs. "The door will shut and we'll finally find out what has been lurking in the shadows."

"Good grief." Maisie rubbed her head and scowled. "It won't hurt it, will it?"

"I don't think so." The grimoire didn't say, but it was a cage . . . not a mousetrap. I grimaced at the thought of it being a mouse. I was not a fan of rodents.

We walked back into the kitchen, and I extracted the poisonous plant book from my bag. Lying it on the counter, Maisie set a box of cereal and a bowl in front of me. As soon as I began shoving fruit loops into my mouth, I started turning pages, scanning the pictures for anything purple.

Almost to the end of the book, and I still hadn't found a plant that resembled the petal I had found. I was getting worried, wondering if I had been wrong. Was it possible the petal wasn't poisonous? Rubbing my thumb and index finger together, I remembered the way they had gone numb.

I turned a page, almost splashing the remaining milk from my bowl as I stood up straight. Wolfsbane. There it was. A match. The petals of the flower shaped like a hood. I set my bowl down and picked up the book, turning to lean my back against the edge of the counter.

"What did you find?" Maisie leaned closer.

I poked the picture. "This is what was in the hardware store."

Every part of the plant was poisonous—including the petals—and it didn't have to be ingested. I ran my finger down the paragraphs, absorbing all the information it offered, slowing at the mythology of the plant.

Wolfsbane was used to repel werewolves. *Werewolves?* I glanced at Maisie. She was reading along, her brows furrowed. I closed my eyes, thinking about the wolves running around Wildewood. They had been large, bigger than I had expected. Was it possible . . . No. I closed the book and laid it on the counter. Werewolves, really?

"Riley, you don't think that has anything to do with the murders, do you?"

I rubbed my temple in a circular motion. "God, I hope not." The thought of werewolves was terrifying. Any movie I had ever seen told me werewolves were bad news. I wanted to rule it out altogether, but we had just set a trap for a hobgoblin. We were witches, and we had a ghost for an aunt. At this point, anything was possible.

But, seriously, werewolves?

Chapter 29

Bean never came home, and he never appeared on our way to the café. I grew more concerned over him missing with the possibility of werewolves running around Wildewood. I had trouble sleeping not knowing if he was safe. But he had to be okay—he just had to be. There had to be a good reason why he wasn't hanging around. Agatha probably had him on some mission. If she would ever pop back in, I would ask her.

Werewolves in Wildewood. I wanted to dismiss the notion, but I had seen them with my own eyes. Of course, at the time I didn't know that's what they were. I figured they were just overgrown wolves. But in this weird town, I couldn't rule anything out.

Maisie pushed through the kitchen door with a fresh batch of blueberry scones. Zach stood across the room taking an order from a couple who had just sat down. I closed the register and handed the woman in front of me a receipt, barely hearing her say goodbye. I had too much on my mind; too many questions, and not enough answers.

I wanted to know if the Wolfsbane had been used on Sasha

because she was a werewolf. Did that mean Eugene was one too? Rubbing my temples at the formation of a headache, I looked up at the sound of the chime. Connie Fields walked inside. She loosened her mustard-colored scarf from around her neck and pulled a pair of tan gloves from her hands. Her granddaughters, Daisy and Rose, trailed behind her bundled in matching black, puffer jackets that went to mid-thigh.

They styled their light-brown hair the same way: straightened and cut to their shoulders. They both had dark-brown eyes, thin eyebrows, and pale lips. Daisy and Rose did a better job at being twins than Maisie and me. Except, they weren't twins.

I placed three to-go cups on the counter. They always took their coffees to go. Waiting for them to reach me, I decided to ask about Wolfsbane. I had little reason to believe Daisy was involved, but I didn't want to rule her out altogether just yet. She was, after all, the last person to handle the flower arrangement before Sasha died.

"Good morning. Want to try something new today?" I greeted them with a smile.

All three shook their heads.

That was all I needed. I knew their orders by heart. The one thing the girls did differently was their coffee. I made Daisy's Rich Witch, adding extra caramel because that's how she liked it. A Wicked Witch—mint, dark-chocolate Frappuccino—for Rose, and a simple Hocus Focus for Connie because she believed "coffee should taste like coffee."

Handing over the drinks, I wrote out the receipt and decided it was now or never. "Can I ask you a plant question?"

"Of course, what is it?" Connie stirred a single packet of sweetener into her coffee.

Rose excused herself and hurried toward the bathroom, leaving her drink on the counter.

I leaned closer to Connie, lowering my voice from prying ears. "Do you sell Wolfsbane?"

Daisy coughed, placing her cup on the counter, she covered her mouth. Connie patted her on the back and made an exasperated remark under her breath.

"Good grief." Connie handed her a napkin.

"Sorry." Daisy cleared her throat. "It went down wrong."

With an eye roll, Connie asked, "What was your question?"

"Do you sell Wolfsbane?" I watched Connie's eyes widen, her lips parting. She snapped her mouth shut. Daisy brought her cup back to her mouth, this time successfully taking a sip.

"Heaven's no. Why are you asking?"

Not wanting to tell Connie the true reason why, I asked, "Do you know who does?"

Connie scoffed as she stood. She shook her head, her big, black-rimmed glasses sliding to the tip of her nose. "No one I know, and don't you go around trying to get some. It's dangerous."

I gave her a weak smile and the receipt. I had no plans to grow it or to have anymore in my possession. All I wanted to know was how it came to Wildewood. Who would bring in something so deadly?

Rose walked back to the counter and picked up her to-go cup, none the wiser to our conversation as she smiled. She took the receipt from Connie and checked out with Maisie. Daisy's cheeks were flushed, though I wasn't sure if it was from choking on her coffee or my line of questions.

"Daisy, go wait at the door for me," Connie commanded,

then zoned in on me. "Riley Jones, I've only ever known one person to grow Wolfsbane, and now, they're dead."

She turned away before I had a chance to ask who. Catching up with her granddaughters, she held the door open for them and took one last glimpse at me before stepping out of the café. They walked across the street, the wind rustling Connie's silver hair. Was she talking about Sasha? Is that why Sasha had checked out the book? Had she grown the plant that ultimately killed her?

"Everything okay?" Maisie nudged me with her elbow. She was following my gaze out the window, but Connie and her granddaughters were already across the street. I wish I knew exactly who she had been referring to. Maybe if I got her alone, without any prying ears, she'd fill me in. Connie loved to gossip as much as Pete loved sweets. I only hoped she couldn't resist.

"Yeah. Everything's fine."

Everything was fan-freakin-tastic. What could possibly be wrong this Christmas? Bean was still missing and wolves were in Wildewood. Sasha had been murdered by the very thing she seemed to have been researching or growing. Eugene was missing and Wolfsbane was in the hardware store. He and Sheriff Vargas had been in a more or less public argument over Peaceful Acres.

Ah—maybe that's what I needed to focus on—the issue with Peaceful Acres.

Chapter 30

Grabbing my coat and the last blueberry scone, I made my way to the large office building where Wildewood Realty resided. Ethan wouldn't be picking us up to take us to Peaceful Acres until late afternoon. That gave me a few hours to talk to Natalie Remington, get home, and get ready.

I pushed the door open to the office building and walked to the directory sign in the middle of the lobby. The last time I was here I had been searching for answers about the murder of the Mayor's almost-son-in-law. Here I was again, searching for answers. Thankfully, this time, I didn't have to walk up four flights of stairs. Wildewood Realty was located on the main floor.

I walked through the lobby, past the elevators, and around a corner to the right. I heard a door open and Sophia King, Vargas' niece, walked into the hallway. She was staring at her phone, grumbling under her breath. I looked around for any place to hide but unfortunately, there wasn't a nook or cranny for me to shove into until she passed.

She turned her back to me, an arm crossed over her stomach, the other held a phone to her ear. "Hey. We have a problem."

She turned around. Her eyes widened, and she quickly hung up her call. "Good morning." She nodded and strolled down the hallway. I watched her until she turned the corner.

I continued toward the office door Sophia had just come out of and pulled it open to step into a sepia-toned room. The waiting area felt more like an outdated doctor's office. Brown chairs lined one wall, and above them were dozens of pictures of happy, smiling faces holding keys and shaking hands with various realtors who work here. I tapped the little bell on the empty receptionist desk then walked over to inspect the pictures closer when the door into the waiting room opened.

"Can I help you?" Natalie looked at her watch. The tie holding back her wiry brown hair was losing the battle as strands hung loosely around her face. "We are about to close for lunch."

I extended my hand to shake hers and held out the to-go box with the scone inside. "I just had a quick question."

The exasperated look on her face disappeared as she looked inside the box. "Well, I only have a minute. Follow me to my office while I grab my things."

I walked behind her down a brightly lit hallway, the walls the same sepia tone as the waiting room. A large picture of a mansion hung on the wall between her office and the bathroom. I stopped to look at it. The mansion looked familiar but I couldn't place it. I don't think I had ever seen it in Wildewood.

"What's your question?" She patted me on the arm, and I jumped. She had her purse on her shoulder and a scone in her hand.

"Oh." I shook my head to refocus. "I was wondering if you could tell me anything about Peaceful Acres."

She snorted. "Goodness. Peaceful Acres sure is popular these days."

I followed her back down the hallway and out of the office. "Do you know who owns it?"

"Of course I do." She locked the door and placed a sticky note on the outside that read "Out to lunch."

Turning her attention to me, the sticky note floated to the ground behind her. As we started to walk toward the lobby, I folded my arm behind my back and faked a sneeze, reciting "*Surgere*," and flicked my pointer finger upward. I glanced over my shoulder. The note was back on the door where she had placed it.

"It is my job to know everything about every real estate opportunity in Wildewood." She took a bite of her scone. "Oh, wow. I'm going to have to stop in and get one of these on my way to work now. What were we talking about?" she asked.

"I'll make sure to set one aside for you." I jogged to catch up with her. "Peaceful Acres?"

"Right. Peaceful Acres. I hope you aren't looking to buy. The owner is very set on not selling." She opened the door and I walked outside.

"Who is the owner?" I tightened my coat.

Natalie finally stopped moving. I wondered if this was how she always was—nonstop. "Eugene Fletcher. Though, if he isn't found, the property will revert to his son."

What? The words went in one ear and out the other. Feeling speechless, I scooped my jaw off the floor and chased after her.

"He has a great opportunity to make quite a fortune if he sells. There's a willing buyer too. But"—she shrugged, dusting crumbs from her hands—"you just can't force it."

"Who wants to buy it?" I knew the answer, but I wanted to hear it from her mouth.

"Manuel Vargas. But, hey, I gotta get going. I have about half an hour to wolf down lunch before my next client shows up. Remember my name if you're ever in the market to sell or buy." She gave me a large, toothy smile, and I had a feeling that was the smile reserved for clients only.

I stood under the overhang of the building, trying to digest the information Natalie had given me. The two men weren't in business with each other. The sheriff wanted Eugene's land. Ethan had been the one to tell me that. My jaw tensed, thinking about Ethan keeping things from me. Why hadn't he just said that?

Everything had to do with this land. There was something about Peaceful Acres that was worth killing over. At this point, I was starting to believe Eugene was dead. I just didn't understand what was so important about Peaceful Acres.

I felt a headache coming on. Maisie had been right; I should've just left this to the fine police of Wildewood to figure out. Except . . . would the sheriff interfere? What if it got back to him and he put a stop to the investigation? Could he even do that?

Of course he could.

I started to walk toward home, a chill rushing over me. If Eugene wasn't already dead, were they torturing him until he finally agreed to give up his land? Oh, God. That's why Michael ran. If Eugene died, they would go after him.

My stomach sank and my heart began to hurt. I needed to get to Peaceful Acres as soon as possible. Maybe then I would understand the importance because right now, I had just added a ton more to my list of I don't knows.

Chapter 31

I heard Ethan's truck purr as it pulled into the driveway. I rubbed my head against Bean's, thankful he was home and safe. He had shown up right when we got off work. Maisie pulled her jacket on, her hair waterfalling over her shoulders. Setting Bean down, I stood from my perch on the steps and slid my thicker, black jacket on over my sweater. Bean rubbed against Maisie's leg until she scooped him up, nuzzling his soft fur.

Ethan nudged the door open, poking his head inside. His lips twitched into a smile. "Ready to go?" He glanced at Maisie. "Hey! He finally showed back up."

He reached out to pet him but decided against it and tucked his arm back to his side. Ethan liked Bean, but he had learned his lesson when trying to pet him. Bean had made it very clear, numerous times, that he did not reciprocate the same feelings.

I locked the door behind us. Maisie, still holding Bean, rushed ahead and climbed into the back seat of the truck.

"Are you sure you guys want a real tree?" Ethan wrapped his hand around mine as we walked to the driveway.

I gave him a side glance. "I'm sure." I knew he didn't want

us going, but I wanted to see Peaceful Acres for myself. I wanted to see what was so special about it, if anything. There had to be a reason why people were being killed over it—not that there was ever a good excuse for murder.

He opened my door, closing it after I slid onto the seat, then jogged to the other side. The truck was still warm as he backed out of the driveway. I could hear Bean purring behind me and Maisie whispering in a baby voice. I couldn't help but smile. We were finally getting one thing done for Christmas, even if I had ulterior motives.

We drove through Wildewood, past all the little shops decorated for Christmas, and headed toward the bridge separating our town from the rest of the world. The roads were slick with snow turning into slush. The trees looked crystallized as the temperature dropped.

Before we reached the bridge, Ethan turned onto a gravel road and we drove under a wooden arch with a metal sign, letting us know we had arrived. The half-mile drive to the tree farm was the only cleared land before we reached a small, red barn.

Ethan parked the truck in front of it. I climbed out, opening the door for Maisie. Newly planted firs were in neat little rows just behind the barn. The further back, the larger the trees, until the forest took over.

"Let me grab a saw." Ethan pointed to the barn. Half a dozen saws hung from the sidewall with a sign that said "Cut your own tree."

I walked to the shed and poked my head inside to see if anyone was home. There was a handwritten note on the counter that said "Be back soon," and signed with only an *S*. I guess we were on our own for the moment.

Walking through the trees, my nerves began to vibrate—except, I wasn't nervous, not really. The sensation started in my feet, running up my legs, and I wondered if it was the land that caused it. A frigid gust of wind ruffled my hair, and I pulled my hood on. I glanced at Ethan, noting how gold his eyes looked. His thick, fleece-lined jacket was unzipped and I wasn't sure how he could stand the cold.

Bean padded in front of us, leaving small paw prints in the snow, his little bell jingling louder in the silence as we walked toward the back rows of fir trees. Maisie pointed to a tree that had to be at least seven feet tall.

"Looks good." I smiled at her, pulling my hood tighter around my face. It was getting colder, and I didn't want to be in the woods when it got dark. Feeling a little disappointed that there hadn't been a big ah-ha moment, and the secrets of Peaceful Acres revealed as I had hoped, I was ready to go.

We stood back as Ethan got to work sawing the base of the trunk. Snow flittered off the branches as the tree swayed. Bean started to walk further into the denser trees. I jogged to catch him, not wanting to lose him. He finally stopped ahead of me when his paw stepped into a print much larger than his own. Bean turned his head to look up at me as if he was trying to tell me something. Now would be a good time to talk. I've heard him before, I knew he could, but he stayed silent.

Scooping him up, I crouched, placing my hand in the paw-print. The tips of my fingers just barely hung over the indention. Leaves rustled close by. I spun around, ready to run back to Maisie and Ethan, but a growl came from behind a tree. Bean clawed my arm, forcing me to drop him. His back arched, his fur sticking straight up as he hissed. I looked around to see what had him spooked and sucked in a breath as a large, dark-red wolf stepped into view.

Our eyes locked. Its lips pulled back to expose long, powerful teeth as a deep snarl wrapped around me, saliva hanging from its mouth. I took a step back, and it growled again. I couldn't think. I was a damn witch, but I froze. I was scared to move, or do anything to anger it further.

It was double the size of any wolf I had ever seen—except the one that had raced past me near Ethan's. I swallowed, realizing this wasn't an ordinary wolf. This was a real-life werewolf. Bean raced past it and I screamed, taking a step forward, but the wolf reared back on its haunches. Its powerful legs pushed its body forward into the air. It crashed into me, forcing me to the ground.

My head hit something hard, my vision blackening around the edges and a loud ringing vibrated between my ears. I felt something rip through my jeans and pierce my thigh. I was stuck, unable to move without hot pain tearing through my leg. My scream was trapped in my throat, bile rose, and hot tears streamed down my cheeks. The wolf had its powerful jaw wrapped around my leg and there was nothing I could do.

Another growl came from somewhere else and the wolf pulled its teeth from my thigh with a wet sound that made me want to vomit. Blood seeped from holes in my jeans, the white snow turning crimson under me. With its attention diverted, I sucked in a breath, and using only my arms, I dragged myself away. I gasped from the pain as it turned searing and sharp.

The wolf turned around, and I glanced past its large body; its attention was on Ethan. He stood between two trees, the saw falling from his hand. I opened my mouth to tell him to run when he dropped to his knees. He fell forward onto his hands, his back arched, and a piercing cry tore through him.

His body morphed, his limbs growing longer, more muscular, as he transformed into something otherworldly. He threw his head back, a pained howl bellowed from him, and his jaw stretched as it turned into a snout. I would never be able to unsee this, it was forever seared into my brain.

His long body, covered in dark-gray fur, rushed toward the wolf in front of me.

The black edges of my vision grew. Another wolf jumped over me and then all I heard was the wet tearing of flesh and the snapping of jaws. I fell back onto the hardened snow, desperately trying to not throw up. Rolling my head to the side, Maisie knelt beside me. Her mouth moved, a deep line between her brows, but I couldn't hear what she was saying. Tears were running down her cheek. I looked back up to the darkening sky, blinking slowly. The ringing in my ears became deafening as my vision went black.

Chapter 32

Slowly opening my eyes, I found myself staring up at dim fluorescent lights. A machine was beeping at a steady rhythm nearby. The room smelled sterile but there was a vanilla scent hovering around me. My eyelids fluttered, heavy with sleep. The image of a gray wolf appeared, treading toward me. Its cold snout nudged me awake, the musky vanilla scent strengthened. The wolf's baby-blue eyes blinked.

Ethan.

I gasped, my eyes popped open.

"She's awake!" Maisie's face came into view above me.

Trying to sit up, pain slammed into the back of my head and I fell back onto the soft pillow.

I licked my dry lips, my throat even drier. "Where am I?"

"Wildewood Memorial," Ethan answered and wrapped his hand around mine. I looked at his hand, half expecting to see a paw. My gaze wandered to his eyes, and the memory of his face distorting into the wolf made me pull my hand away, causing him to wince.

Maisie wiped a tear from her cheek. "I am so glad you're okay. We were so scared."

She grabbed a remote lying next to my leg, leaning the bed up with a push of a button. Ethan poured water into a Styrofoam cup then handed it to me as he sat on the edge of the bed. I looked at him, feeling hesitant to take the cup.

"I am so sorry you had to find out this way."

I didn't know how to respond. His eyes were cast down, his shoulders sagged. I resisted the urge to pull away again as his hand gripped mine uncomfortably tight. Licking my dry lips, I realized that his secret was much scarier than mine. I understood why he didn't want me to know. He was still Ethan, even if he turned furry occasionally. My fingers brushed his jawline, I didn't like seeing him so distraught. He could've tried to tell me, but how would that have gone? I'm not sure I would've believed him.

"At least I know now." I decided to say and tried to scoot closer to him but a sharp pain stopped me. I pushed the blanket off, exposing a thick, white bandage wrapped around the majority of my thigh. The memory of the red wolf sinking its teeth into me flashed before my eyes. Bile rose into my throat and I sucked in a breath.

"Who were the other two?"

The door to the room started to open and a nurse walked in.

Ethan and Maisie moved to stand in front of the window. The name tag clipped on the pocket of the nurse's lavender scrubs read "Ashley." She took the cup from me and placed it on a tray, swiveling it over the bed. "It's good to see you awake. We were all worried there for a moment. You received your first rabies shot." She touched a bruise on my upper arm. "We are going to keep you overnight, just in case. I'll be back with some food."

She piddled around for a moment, checking my vitals, and when she was satisfied with the numbers, turned the machine off and left the room.

I looked at Ethan. "The other two wolves?"

He rubbed his hand over his mouth. "Michael." He shook his head, his hand falling back to his side. "I don't know who the other one was. I know it was female, but for some reason, it had no scent."

Something was masking its scent? "How is that possible?" When I looked at Ethan, he only shrugged. I had a feeling it had something to do with Wolfsbane. It was the only connection. But I was feeling a bit hesitant about asking any more questions. Whoever the other wolf was, they were not happy about me sticking my nose where it didn't belong.

"I'm going to run home and pack an overnight bag for you." Maisie brushed a strand of hair behind my ears. "Will you be okay?"

What could possibly happen to me in a crowded hospital?

"I'll give you a ride." Ethan pulled his keys out of his pocket and I realized he was wearing a different outfit. "Unless"—he looked at me—"you want me to stay."

Before I could answer, Maisie held her hand out over the bed. Ethan dropped the keys into her palm. "I promise I'll be as quick as possible." She rushed out of the room, and I sighed, realizing I had lost two pairs of pants this week.

"Can I sit beside you?" Ethan asked.

It was a bizarre thing to ask for two people that were dating. But I could tell he was worried I was scared of him. And I was, a little. But he's still Ethan, I reminded myself. Gritting my teeth, I moved closer to the side of the bed, so Ethan could sit. He climbed beside me, barely having enough room. Leaning against his shoulder, his arm wrapped behind my neck, I looked up at him, his eyes were locked on the bandage on my thigh. Guilt must be eating him up.

I placed my hand on his. "Ethan, even if you had told me, it wouldn't have changed what happened."

"You don't know that." His thumb caressed my knuckles.

I kissed his jaw. "I'm okay." The pain in my thigh screamed otherwise, but I was alive and he had saved me from a far worse fate.

The door to the room opened and I figured it was the nurse with whatever food she had promised. I was hoping for Jello, any flavor besides lime. Though, I was hungry enough that I'd happily eat it.

"Would you hurry?" Esther Miller backed into the room, holding the door open for Connie Fields.

Shit. Definitely not Jello.

"Oh, Riley!" Connie rushed to the bed. "Don't worry. We are going to take care of you."

Ethan moved, standing a few feet away from the bed. Connie sat near my knee. "Take care of me?" I was in the hospital, being taken care of by a nurse. What more could they possibly do? I looked at Ethan, begging him to explain what they were talking about.

"Come on." Esther motioned her hand toward the door. Connie pulled the blanket off me, exposing my legs. I pulled the hospital gown down. "Hurry up, now."

Very slowly, I swung my legs over the bed and looked around for anything that could cover my backside before I stood. "What's going on?"

I tied the lower tie on the back of the gown as tight as I could. Ethan grabbed his jacket from a chair and laid it on my shoulders. Esther picked up my boots beside the door and brought them to the bed. I couldn't bring my leg up to shove my foot inside without nauseating pain rushing over me. Maybe I would just go barefoot. Ethan took the boots and slid them over the thick hospital socks for me.

"Thanks," I whispered to him. He pulled me up off the bed, but I could barely put any weight on my leg, so I clung to him. "Can one of you please tell me what we're doing?" And maybe get me a wheelchair because there was no way in Hell I'd be able to walk to the parking lot.

"We have to make sure you aren't infected." Connie ushered me to the door.

What the hell? I gripped Ethan's sweater, forcing him to stop. "Infected with what?" I had already gotten one round of the rabies shot. I swear I'd come back for the other ones.

Ethan, realizing how badly I was limping, gently picked me up and carried me past them. I could feel a breeze where the gown was hanging open under me. "Come on. I'll explain in the car."

Esther told us to go as she pulled the door closed. No one seemed to notice our movements toward the stairs. I wondered if she was working some magic to aid in our escape, but it wasn't like any machines were screaming since I'd gotten out of the bed.

"Quickly." Connie rushed down the stairs. "We have a short time frame after a bite."

As if I weighed nothing, Ethan walked down the stairs with me in his arms. I glanced up at him, expecting to see the sheen of sweat on his forehead, instead, all I saw was worry. His breathing was steady—so much about him was starting to make sense.

"Wait—" I gripped his shoulders a little tighter. "Am I going to turn into a . . ."

"A werewolf? Well,"—Connie hurried him with a wave of her hand—"not if I can get my poultice on you as soon as possible." Was this a joke? She pushed us through the emergency exit and the alarm began to ring loudly. "Whoopsie. Hurry, now."

"She's not serious, right?"

Ethan's Adam's apple bobbed, his lips drawn thin.

Fuck.

Connie's delivery van was parked illegally outside of the hospital. Ethan pulled the back door open and I grunted as I scooted backward into it. As soon as he closed the doors, Connie sped out of the parking lot. I fell into Ethan and he helped prop me back up. The slip-proof padding lining the van was not helping to keep me steady.

"Wait. What about Esther?" Ethan yelled toward the front of the van.

A little snort came from me. Esther had a way of getting around that I did not personally enjoy. I had experienced it once before, and as uncomfortable as I was at the moment, I was glad we were sitting in the back of Connie's van, surrounded by flowers.

Chapter 33

Connie slammed on the brakes in front of my house, and I fell into a container of red carnations. Mumbling obscenities, I pushed myself back up into a sitting position. The jerky movement made my thigh hurt worse and I feared I had ripped open stitches.

Trying to keep my hurt leg straight, I scooted toward the edge of the van where Ethan waited. He picked me up, this time making sure my gown wasn't hanging open for all the neighbors to see, and carried me toward the house. Now I understood where his strength came from. I knew he ran every morning and worked out most days, but it all made sense now.

His truck was in the driveway. Maisie stood on the porch with Madam Mayor. Ethan's steps faltered. Confusion flashed across his face as he looked at me. I shrugged. There was more to her than any of us knew. I found that if I just went with it, it would work out better in the end. Better for who was the real question.

Connie strolled past us with a large canvas bag over her shoulder. "Maisie, would you show me to the kitchen."

Maisie exchanged a glance with me before opening the door. Oh, look, we were in the kitchen. I pressed a finger to my lips, stifling a laugh. I either found myself hilarious or I was in a state of delusion from the pain radiating through my thigh. Our house was rather small. The kitchen and living room were one open room. No wonder Ethan had caught on to what we were so quickly. I should've made a 'rule' to not use magic when he was over, but it didn't matter at this point. We both knew each other's secrets, and I was hoping it was for the best.

"I need to make the poultice quick." Connie laid the large tote on the kitchen table.

Ethan sat me on the couch. He propped my leg up with a pillow before sitting on the coffee table. His eyes were focused on the bandage around my thigh. A deep crease formed between his brows. His thumb ran over mine as he held my hand. If he kept doing that, he was likely to rub my skin off.

Noises from the kitchen pulled my attention away. Connie removed half a dozen jars of herbs from her bag. She set a large mortar and pestle beside them then opened a small black book. Even with her coke-bottle glasses, she held the book close to her nose as she read. She made little "Mhmm" noises as she moved the jars around in an order I did not understand.

It didn't surprise me to find out Connie was a witch. In fact, it explained a lot of things about her that I had always wondered about.

Agatha appeared beside Connie; her arms crossed under her chest. She was more corporeal than normal. "We have a better recipe in the Wildewood grimoire."

"Hello, Agatha." Connie didn't even flinch.

They knew each other, and that didn't surprise me either.

Agatha and my mother had grown up in Wildewood. Agatha snapped her fingers and the grimoire, along with the key, floated from Maisie's room toward the table. She unlocked it and flicked her hand over the pages until they opened to what I assumed was a recipe for whatever poultice Connie was in the process of making.

Bean jumped onto the couch and I reached out to rub between his ears. He and Ethan stared at each other for a moment and then something clicked—I understood why Bean didn't like Ethan. Since that mortifying day, covered in flour from head to toe, when Bean came into my life, he had been trying to tell me about Ethan. I just hadn't caught on.

Maisie walked into the living room. I stared at her for a moment then my vision began to swim in a galaxy of stars. My head fell backward. I yanked at Ethan's jacket, trying to remove it. My forehead was soaked in sweat. My skin felt as if it were on fire. Bile crept up my throat and I heard Maisie's voice but it sounded distant.

"Are you okay?" She knelt beside me, her hands touching my arm. They were so cold.

I tried to shake my head, but the movement curdled my stomach. I cried out. The wound on my thigh burned, more intense than when the wolf had first bit me.

A plume of smoke came from the kitchen table. Connie fanned it away. The back-and-forth motion made me dizzier.

I looked at Ethan. "Something's wrong."

He jumped to his feet. "Connie!"

Were we too late? I guess I wouldn't need that second rabies shot after all.

Chapter 34

Sun filtered through the curtains as I blinked my eyes open. I started to push myself up, immediately hissing from the pain in my thigh. Tears stung my eyes and I laid back down, staring up at the ceiling as I waited for the pain to subside. I turned my head and spotted a note lying on the coffee table, then looked at Ethan who was sleeping in the chair beside the couch, his legs dangling over the arm.

I reached over to grab the note. My fingers touched the corner and I slid it closer. It was from Maisie. She and Zach would take care of the café and asked me not to worry and to stay in bed. She should be aware by now that I have trouble following orders. I tossed the note back on the table.

My throat was dry, my head ached. I forced myself to sit up. Putting all my weight on my left leg, I stood, then hobbled to the kitchen. I filled a glass of water and drank it so quickly that it ran down my chin onto the hospital gown.

I pulled the hem of the gown up and looked at the new bandage Connie had wrapped around my thigh. I could see a hardened, black substance around the edges, barely remembering her applying the poultice. Though I do remember her telling me to leave it on for twenty-four hours, otherwise, it wouldn't work.

I planned to heed her warning. I didn't know how the poultice could help, but I would try anything to not become a werewolf. A laugh escaped my throat. A fucking werewolf.

I wiped the water from my chin and heard the chair in the living room squeak. Ethan swung his feet to the floor. He raised his arms over his head and stretched out his back. As I watched, I wondered how he'd become a werewolf. Had he been bitten? Was he born that way?

A shiver ran through me and I realized I wasn't on fire anymore. I was cold and the hospital gown was once again gaping in the back. Thank goodness the kitchen blinds were closed, otherwise, my neighbors might have seen a different kind of full moon. Ethan groaned as he rose from the chair. He mosied over, still looking concerned as if he wasn't sure I was free and clear yet. I mentally rolled my eyes, feeling as if we were waiting on STD results. Of all the things, I never would have thought to ask a new partner if he was a werewolf . . .

"How are you feeling?" he said groggily, running his hands over his face.

"Cold." I set the cup in the sink. "Do you think you could grab a change of clothes for me?" I wasn't sure I could climb the stairs yet. "There's a pair of sweats near the hamper."

He placed a kiss on the top of my head and returned promptly with the WPD sweats in his hands as I hobbled back to the couch. His hands were warm against my skin as he helped untie the back of the hospital gown. His fingers trailed down my back, and I winced when they touched various bruises from my fall. His lips were soft against my shoulder as I pulled the gown off and let it drop to the floor.

I pulled a sports bra on over my head, then the big, dark-blue sweater. These were becoming more handy than I expected. Grabbing the sweatpants, I realized I wouldn't be able to bend my leg to slip them on. Ethan took them from me, kneeled, and helped me into them.

"A lot of things make sense now," I whispered, filling the silence between us.

"Yeah? Like what?" He grabbed the gown off the floor and walked into the kitchen to throw it away.

"Like why your eyes sometimes turn gold, your strength . . ." I slowly lowered onto the couch. "Is there anything I should know about witches and wolves being together?"

Ethan had this ability to invade my senses, to cause me not to think straight. His scent was intoxicating to me and I wondered if it was because of what we were. He walked back to me and took my hands in his as he sat on the coffee table. His lips grazed my knuckles.

"Nothing you need to worry about."

He stood abruptly, my hands falling into my lap. He looked toward the front door. Someone knocked. He told me to stay as if I was going anywhere. Then it dawned on me that Ethan had heard the person behind the door before they'd had a chance to knock. Did he have exceptional hearing, or was this a side effect of being a werewolf?

He walked to the front door and a moment later, Michael stepped into view. He looked at me, his face going slack, and made his way toward me. "I am so sorry." Michael sat on the edge of the coffee table where Ethan had just been, shaking his head slightly.

"I don't remember anything after the wolf attacked me, but I have a feeling I owe you a thank you." I offered a weak smile.

"Actually, you owe it to Maisie."

"Maisie?" I glanced at Ethan, my stomach knotting at the thought of Michael seeing her use magic.

He nodded, plopping into the chair he had slept on.

"Not sure what she did, but it scared it off," Michael added.

Relief flooded me, knowing Michael hadn't seen anything. I wasn't ready for any more people to know what we were.

I looked down at my leg, even though I couldn't see the bandage anymore, and rubbed a hand over it gently. I wondered what Maisie had done. She was strong, but I assumed she hadn't killed the wolf. Someone would have told me, right? I mean, surely, they wouldn't hide that from me.

Glancing between the two men, my gaze rested on Michael. "Do you know who the other wolf is?"

He shook his head and I sighed. Something had prevented these two from recognizing its scent.

Michael shifted, growing uncomfortable. He licked his lips and stood, walking to the other side of the coffee table. I eyed him. Whatever he needed to say, he felt the need to put distance between us. "I need your help."

"With what?" What could I possibly offer right now in my . . . current condition?

"I need your magic."

My mouth opened. How the hell did he know? I jerked my head toward Ethan, and he shook his head. "How do you— who told you?"

Michael raised an eyebrow, looking between Ethan and me for a moment, then answered in a matter-of-fact tone, "I can smell it. All wolves can smell a witch."

Dealing with the pain, I stood and dragged myself to stand in front of Ethan. "Is that how you knew? You could smell my magic?"

Ethan stared at his hands in his lap.

Seriously? "Did you know the whole time?"

My heart sank as he sat there, silent. He had known the moment we ran into each other? Ethan wouldn't look at me. I shook my head, nostrils flaring, and turned away from him. Gritting my teeth, I headed toward the kitchen. I knew it didn't matter anymore, but it hurt to know he had led me to believe it was my own ineptitude that caused him to find out about my magic.

I could feel him behind me, his vanilla scent muskier.

"If I had told you the real reason I found out, I would've had to tell you—"

I swung around to face him, my thigh screaming in retaliation. "The truth!" Tears stung my eyes.

"Can you two please do this later?" Michael interrupted, and anger bubbled inside of me. Good thing I wasn't turning into a dragon, otherwise, Michael would be toast. He held his palms out. "I don't have a lot of time before it's too late."

Closing my eyes, I took a deep breath then exhaled slowly. It didn't matter, I repeated to myself. I knew now. Forcing my temper down, I locked onto Michael. "How do you want me to help?"

"I need you to do a location spell."

I would do it, but I wasn't doing it because he asked, or even if Ethan asked. I would do it to help Eugene. If there was a chance he could still be alive, I would do anything to help find him. Except . . . I had no idea how to do a location spell.

"Maybe Esther can help me figure out—"

"No," Michael snapped. "I need *your* help."

"Esther would—"

Michael took my hand, and there was a zap of energy between us. I looked up into his dark-brown eyes and watched them turn golden. "You don't have a claim in wolf matters. Esther does."

I chewed on my bottom lip, feeling uncertain. I wasn't sure how Esther, a witch, could have a claim in wolf matters, but then again Esther had her nose in everyone's business. Not only was she the mayor, but she was also a Keeper. I suppose it made sense that she played a part in their business too.

"Okay. I'll figure it out. But"—I limped away from them to sit at the kitchen table with a dull, angry ache running through my leg—"before I do anything, I want some answers."

Impatience flashed over Michael's face, but he sighed and sat beside me. Even if he didn't answer my questions, I'd help, but I wanted him to believe I had the upper hand.

"Where does your father fit into all of this?" Michael was a werewolf, so I felt it was safe to assume his father was too. But I didn't understand why he and Vargas were fighting over Peaceful Acres. If Eugene didn't want to sell it, who cared?

"My father is the alpha of the Wildewood pack."

Oh. "And Vargas?"

"He wants control," Ethan answered.

I swallowed. Vargas was a werewolf too. "How does another wolf gain control?"

"Either the current alpha surrenders or they take it by force."

Ethan crossed his arms over his chest and leaned against the island.

"And Peaceful Acres—what does it have to do with the pack?" Even though my leg ached, I decided to busy myself with making coffee. I knew Ethan could use some, and the dark circles under Michael's eyes told me he could too. As for me, not even coffee was going to make me feel better right now.

"We use the land during full moons. It's safer than being in town. As long as I've been alive, whoever the alpha is, controls the land, but . . ." Michael leaned back in his chair. "My father was trying to change the rules. He didn't want the land getting into the wrong hands, so he put it in his will. If he dies, the land goes to me."

That explains why Michael has been hiding. If it reverts to him, he really would be in trouble. It did make me wonder who all knew about this exchange. Obviously the wolf pack, but who else was a wolf?

I ran my fingers through my hair, pushing it away from my forehead. "So, your father was trying to change pack rules . . . but why does it matter who has control?" I still didn't understand. I pressed the button on the coffee maker and it began to brew.

"It's just the way it is." Ethan scooted past me to grab a few mugs from the cabinet.

"I know what my father was doing goes against pack policy, but someone else is breaking the rules. They're killing off pack members to suit their needs." Meaning Sasha was a wolf. "They're overthrowing the alpha without a fair fight!" Michael slammed his fist on the table.

I jumped at the sound and pressed my back against the

counter. He was breathing heavily, his eyes glistening. I hadn't meant to upset him; I was only trying to understand.

I remembered the conversation I'd eavesdropped on between Eugene and Michael. He had tried to convince his father nothing had changed. But now, as I looked at him, I knew he hadn't believed it. He knew his father was putting himself in danger by changing the way the land changed hands. Eugene was doing it for a reason though, and I think he knew Vargas was going to challenge him. Was this his way of avoiding it? Or was there a more sinister reason?

Michael laid his hand flat on the table. His chest rose and fell as he calmed himself down. "That son of a bitch got his wife killed because of how badly he wants possession of Peaceful Acres."

I looked at Ethan. "Vargas killed his own wife?" He couldn't have. He was next to the buffet table the whole time he was at the Christmas party.

"No, but I bet he knows who did. They're not working alone." Michael bared his teeth as he spoke.

"Sasha was vocal in her opposition of her husband trying to become alpha," Ethan added. "She knew he wouldn't make it."

Standing, Michael peered down at me. "Unless he cheats. Will you help me?"

I nodded. "I will."

He gave a quick nod to Ethan then walked to the front door. "Please don't take too long. I'll be back soon."

Whoever was working with Vargas knew what Wolfsbane could do to werewolves. The mythology I read must be true. If Sasha hadn't been helping her husband, then why had she checked out the poisonous plant book from the library? Had she figured out their plan? Was she trying to stop it, or use it against them?

Ethan handed me a steaming cup of coffee and I stared into the liquid. Without speaking, it rippled. I needed a boost of energy if I was going to be of any help to anyone. The only people I could think of who might be helping Vargas were Jessica Freki or Daisy.

"Ethan, do you know what Daisy is?" I took a sip, the liquid burning my throat.

"Yeah, she's a witch like Connie. Why?"

"Just wondering." I set the cup down and walked into the bathroom.

I turned the water on, letting it run over my fingers as I waited for it to warm up. It felt safe to cross Daisy off my list. Any one of Esther's guests could've brought the Wolfsbane with them . . . but my bet was now on Jessica Freki.

I poked my head out of the bathroom. Ethan was still standing near the coffee pot. He looked up with a raised brow. "Jessica Freki?"

He nodded. "She's a wolf."

After washing my face and brushing my teeth, Ethan carried me up to the loft. He set me gently on my feet and I limped over to the dresser. The poultice had to be healing the wound on my thigh because it didn't hurt as badly as it had an hour ago. Or I'd be turning furry during the next full moon. Guess we'd find out soon.

Grabbing a pair of clean socks, I shut the drawer and the small perfume vial rolled off the dresser. I groaned as I bent to pick it up, my back stiff from sleeping on the couch. I looked at the light-purple liquid as it moved back and forth in the tube.

Jessica had been wearing this for a while, and now that I knew she was a wolf, I wondered if there was more to the perfume than just a terrible smell.

"What's that?" Ethan asked from the edge of the bed.

Giving him a side glance, I pursed my lips. "You tell me."

I dragged myself over to him and unscrewed the top. He backed away, rubbing at his nose. "That smells terrible."

"Yes, it does." I would regret this, but I dabbed the roller ball on my wrist. I took a step away from him and spread my arms out. "What do you smell?"

Ethan sneezed, rubbing his nose. He took a deep breath, and his brows furrowed. "Nothing . . . I mean, I can smell the perfume but . . ." He stood and sniffed the air. His nose twitched but he held back his sneeze. "I can't smell your magic."

I twisted the lid back on and slipped it into the pocket of my oversized sweats. He couldn't smell me, but what I was sure he meant was that he couldn't smell my magic. Could this perfume be muting the smell of the wolf wearing it?

"I need you to take me to Connie's." I glanced at the alarm clock beside the bed. "And then we need to pick up Maisie, so we can do the location spell."

Chapter 35

I slid off the passenger seat of Ethan's truck, making sure to put my weight on my good leg before hopping out of the way to shut the door. Ethan came up beside me, offering his arm.

"I can carry you," he whispered as I wrapped my hand around his bicep.

"That wouldn't be weird at all." I started walking.

Connie's wasn't too far away, but there hadn't been any parking spots closer. I worried about the stitches in my leg. I had been whisked away so quickly I had no idea what shape my thigh was in, and what damage too much walking would do. I was hoping the poultice was acting like a glue.

Ethan helped me over the curb and we slowly made our way past Luna's boutique. Tugging on his arm, I stopped, seeing Sophia outside. She locked the door and then smoothed out a bright pink piece of paper taped on the glass.

She turned toward us, averting her eyes to the ground then brushed past us with a thin, forced smile. Was being unfriendly a family trait? Ethan turned his head to follow her until she crossed the street toward Town Square. I walked up to the paper taped to the door. It was a typed note from Jessica saying she was out sick and apologizing for the store being closed.

Out sick, huh?

"What did Maisie do to the wolf that attacked me?" I lowered my voice as a woman in a long, red pea coat with the belt tied tight around her waist walked past us. I caught myself wondering what she might be. Another witch? A werewolf? I'd be okay with any, except a wererat. Please don't let those exist.

"She threw it." He forced me to start walking again.

"Threw it?"

"Yeah. She said something and moved her arms." He motioned his hand out in front of his body to show me. "And then the wolf went flying."

Had she been studying the grimoire at night? Maisie was a strong witch, that part I knew, but I didn't like the idea of her learning the more harmful spells behind closed doors. I was already worried enough about her being the 'bad' twin. We reached the door to Connie's. I hesitated, glancing back at Luna's. "How quick can werewolves heal?"

"Relatively fast." He pulled the door open.

Connie looked up from her perch at the counter. She pushed her glasses up with the same hand that held a large set of shears. "Why are you out of bed? You didn't rinse off the poultice, did you?" she chided me, pointing the shears my way.

"No. It's still there." I wrinkled my nose and took the shears out of her hand before she poked her eye out. "I need you to take a look at something."

I pulled the perfume sample out of my pocket and laid it in on the counter.

"What's this?" She held it in front of her face, her glasses magnifying her eyes.

"It's perfume from Luna's. But I think it's more than just perfume."

A single brow rose as Connie unscrewed the lid. She put it right under her nose and I grimaced. Sucking in a deep breath, she gagged and then held the vial as far as her arm could reach. "Riley Jones, I think you're onto something." She jumped from her stool and motioned for us to follow her into the back. "Ethan, would you be a dear and lock the front door for me. We don't need anyone coming in during this."

She rushed around the room, grabbing a bowl and a small dropper bottle. Lying them on the counter near the sink, she pinched her nose and poured half the perfume into the bowl.

"You might want to step back, Ethan," she said as she used her teeth to untwist the bottle. Holding the dropper over the bowl, a single drop of the dark liquid fell from the tip.

A plume of smoke rose. Coughing, I fanned it away. Connie took her glasses off and wiped at her watering eyes. Ethan had moved to the other side of the room but his eyes were red and he had a hand covering his nose and mouth.

"What the hell was that?" I asked, pulling the collar of the sweatshirt over my nose.

"Nothing good." Connie poured her concoction into the large utility sink, turning the water on to flush the smell down the drain.

"What exactly does that mean?" I asked, talking through my shirt.

Connie grabbed another bowl and added another drop of the perfume. She held her hands over it and closed her eyes. Smoke began to pour out from under her hands, but this time it didn't explode. She waved her hands upward. "*Ostende*," she whispered.

The gray smoke changed to a light shade of purple. I moved closer, squinting at what I swore was the shape of a skull within the smoke.

Connie put her arm out, stopping me from getting too close. "You don't want to breathe that in." She clapped her hands together and the smoke dissipated. "This is definitely not good. Where did you say you got this from?" She clicked her tongue, shaking her hand.

"From Luna's." I watched as she disposed of it again. "What's in it?"

Connie stopped moving. Taking a book from the shelf above the sink, she flipped it open to a picture of a purple flower. She glanced over her shoulder at Ethan. "Wolfsbane."

Exchanging a look with him, I followed her back into the front of the store. She laid the book on the counter and sat on her stool, her long legs crossed at the knees and a perplexed look on her face. I leaned back against the counter beside her with my arms crossed over my stomach. Ethan wiped at his face with a damp paper towel, his eyes irritated from the smell.

"Why would someone put Wolfsbane in a perfume?"

Connie snapped to attention, her faraway expression replaced with a large smile. Patting me on the arm, she winked. "There is so much for you to learn."

"I know Wolfsbane is poisonous . . ."

"In large doses, Wolfsbane will kill a werewolf or repel them from an area. But if they eat it . . ." She drew her finger over her neck and stuck her tongue out. "However, in just the right dose," she said with her fingers pinched in front of her face, "it can immobilize. This didn't come to Wildewood by chance."

My stomach twisted. Any hope I had left of Eugene being alive dissolved. "Can a werewolf survive Wolfsbane poisoning?"

Connie tapped a finger to her chin, eying me. "Why do you ask?"

Ethan gripped the counter. His knuckles were white as he held himself up. I touched his shoulder and he growled. There was movement under his skin—his muscles twitching. I took a step back, scared he was about to transform into his wolf again.

"Oh, dear." Connie rushed through the door of the back room.

"Ethan, what's wrong?" I whispered, reaching out to touch him again but my hand fell short.

Connie burst back into the room. She grabbed his chin and forced his mouth open just enough to insert a thin dropper. She squeezed the ball at the end, the liquid emptying into his mouth. "He must've breathed too much of it in."

"What's happening to him?" I watched Ethan swallow, his Adam's apple bobbing. He gagged; his eyes closed tight.

"Did I mention just the smell of it can cause hallucinations, upset stomach, nausea, vomiting, dia—"

"No. No, you did not." I wrapped my hand around Ethan's arm, helping him stand back up. "Are you okay?"

He shook his head. "What was that?"

Beaming, Connie held up the tincture. "It's an antidote I've been working on. I haven't had a chance to use it but it seemed to have worked."

An antidote? Why would she be working on an antidote for Wolfsbane? She had told me she didn't know anyone who grew it. No one alive anyway. I closed my eyes and rubbed my temple. No one who was alive . . .

My eyes popped open. "Did someone ask you to make an antidote?"

She pressed her lips together in a thin line, her eyes widening.

"Connie." I pointed my finger at her. "Who asked you to make an antidote?"

She flapped her hand in front of her, letting out a sigh. "Well, I guess it doesn't matter now. I feel so terrible. I hadn't finished it when . . ."

"Who? Connie?"

She rolled her eyes and pushed her glasses to sit on top of her head. "Sasha Vargas."

Taking a step back in disbelief, I stared at the small bottle on the counter. Sasha knew someone was going to use Wolfsbane on the wolves of Wildewood. That's why she checked out the book, she was searching for answers. She must've figured out what was going on and turned to Connie. I wonder if the perfume was being used to subdue her into compliance, and when it wasn't enough, she was silenced.

My thoughts shifted to Eugene. If that antidote had helped Ethan, maybe it could help Eugene—if he was still alive. Connie caught me staring at it and picked up the bottle. Holding it by the rubber top, she tapped it on her palm.

"Do you know something I don't?" she asked me.

Nodding, I glanced at Ethan. "I think Eugene was poisoned, but—" I took a deep breath. "I think he might still be alive." I was being hopeful. I didn't want to give up yet.

"Take it." She held it out across the counter. "I can always make more."

I wrapped my fingers around the smooth glass. If Eugene was still alive, this might be the only thing that would save him. The poison had worked fast on Sasha, but Vargas needed Eugene alive until he gave up Peaceful Acres.

Thanking her, I walked to the door and looked over my shoulder as Connie whispered something into Ethan's ear. He nodded and, in just a few long strides, caught up with me. Connie had her slender arms wrapped around her tall frame. The wrinkles around her mouth deepened as she brought her gaze up to look at us.

"What did she say?"

Ethan brushed a few strands of hair from my face, pushing it behind my ear. "Nothing for you to worry about."

Chapter 36

Ignoring Ethan's pleas for me to get back in the truck, I limped toward the café to wait for Maisie. The chatter from the square was boisterous. Though it was cold, the rays from the sun were warm. I heard his truck growl to life, and I picked up my pace—still slower than I preferred. Trying to push down the feeling of being upset from the secret he and Connie had shared, I needed a moment alone. These people would never learn their secrets were getting people killed.

I have no idea what Sasha had said to Connie when she asked for an antidote. Surely Connie had been curious. But maybe that was just me . . . maybe I hadn't lived in this secret-keeping town long enough to know not to ask questions. I would've wanted to know why, and I probably wouldn't have helped without an answer.

Probably.

My thigh ached as I reached the fence around the patio of the café. It just wasn't in my nature not to be curious. I heard Bean's bell jingle and he jumped over the fence and onto one of the small black tables. Maybe I had been a cat in a past life. I wasn't sure if I even believed in past lives, but I knew I did not have nine lives, and I had gotten too close to death these last few months.

Just one secret after another, from the moment I stepped foot in this town. Hell, my whole life had been a secret. We had been a secret kept from my father. My magic was a secret I had kept from everyone. Every person in this town had a secret and look what was happening. Nothing good.

Rubbing under Bean's chin, I wondered what he was hiding from me. He opened his eyes to look at me. I probably didn't want to know. Maisie walked out of the door, her back turned to me as she locked it. Turning around, her eyes widened when she realized I was in front of her. "Why aren't you in bed?"

"I had an errand to run. I figured we'd pick you up on the way back home."

"Who's we?" She looked around, confused, seeing that I was alone.

Ethan pulled up in front of the café and her lips formed an *O*.

"Come on. We have work to do." I pulled open the passenger door before Ethan had a chance to get out and help. Maisie grabbed Bean from the table and slid in behind me. "Michael stopped by this morning."

"Oh?" She leaned forward, between the two front seats. "Where has he been?"

I shrugged, trying to twist around in my seat but my leg wasn't having it. "He needs us to do a location spell."

Looking at her in the rearview mirror, surprise spread over her face, and then her brows scrunched. "He knows we're witches? I didn't think he saw . . ."

I ran a hand over my face; I had a lot of explaining to do. I started with Michael being a werewolf, which didn't shock her as much as I thought it would. Though, it was possible Ethan had already told her while I laid unconscious in the hospital. However, telling her Eugene was the alpha of the pack did. There had to be more witches in Wildewood, besides us, the mayor, and Connie, but for some reason, he felt we were the only ones who could be trusted in finding his father. Was that a complement?

I bared my teeth in a hiss, the truck bouncing us as it pulled into the driveway. I had been on my leg too much already, I could tell by the burning sensation starting to flare back up. But I couldn't rest yet. We had to get the grimoire and figure out how to locate Eugene before he was poisoned to the point of no return.

"I can't believe someone is poisoning your pack," Maisie said to Ethan as we got out of the truck.

Bean ran up the steps, and as he reached the top he hissed. The fur on his arched back stood on end. Ethan jogged past us but abruptly stopped when he reached the steps. Even though Bean protested with a guttural cry, he grabbed the little cat and carried him back to Maisie.

"Get back in the truck." He pulled his cell phone out of his pocket and dialed a number.

I backed up, glancing at Maisie. "What's going on?"

With the phone held to his ear, he motioned to the truck. "Hey, we have a problem . . . Wolfsbane . . . Yeah, at Riley's." He poked the screen of his phone and slipped it back into his pocket. "I'm going to check the house. Stay here."

Ethan walked under the empty carport to the door off the kitchen. I ignored his request, because that's what I was good at these days, and walked toward the porch steps. Maisie fell in stride behind me but we both stopped, just as Ethan had.

A bundle of Wolfsbane, tied with a twine cord, lay on the doormat.

It was a warning.

Whoever attacked me, whoever was behind the murder of Sasha and Eugene's kidnapping, had placed a warning for us to back off.

"The house is fine. Come on." Ethan walked up behind us.

I jumped, crying out in pain. "Who did you call?" I asked.

"Come on, let's get inside." He picked me up, one arm going under my knees and the other around my back.

I looked up at the brooding expression on his face. "Show off," I whispered.

The corner of his lip twitched, his dimple appearing. His vanilla scent wrapped around me, the heat from his body warming me. I reached up, trailing my fingers over his dimple he was trying to hide. A smile slowly spread over his mouth, and I desperately wanted his lips against mine. My face flushed and I closed my eyes. Was this a side effect of the bite? As much as I enjoyed the heightened attraction I felt for Ethan, I was starting to wonder if the poultice was working.

I was on fire and the only way to quench it was to drag Ethan to my room.

He set me on my feet in the kitchen, my head swooned and I grabbed onto the counter before my knees buckled. His hand pressed against my back to help steady me. I held a finger up; I just needed a moment to screw my head on straight. I didn't know what just happened, but it felt like I had my own animal inside and *it* wanted *his*. I slinked over to the kitchen sink and turned the water on. It felt like ice against my heated skin.

I could still feel him behind me and for just a few minutes—I'd kick myself for this later—I needed him to put some distance between us. And as if it were a Christmas miracle, a knock came at the door. I let out a breath as he moved to answer it.

Chapter 37

John Russell sat across the table from me. He laid his hat beside him, and I could hear the crinkle of a large paper bag that held the Wolfsbane as he moved his legs. He had his little notepad in front of him and a pen in his hand that he clicked over and over as he stared at me.

Leaning against the back of the chair, my arms crossed, I locked eyes with him. I looked him over, realizing I had never seen him smile. Ethan explained to me that he was the pack enforcer, working to keep things orderly when anyone stepped out of line.

And someone stepped out of line big time.

Problem was, the sheriff was also a wolf and was pulling the strings. He had to be careful, otherwise, he could lose his job on the police force, which apparently, he took very seriously. As serious as he took his "Earl Grey, to go," and sneered at any offering of a muffin.

"Can we trust him?" I looked over my shoulder at Ethan, who was leaning against the sink.

He nodded.

"Do you know what's going on?" I leaned forward. "What's *really* going on?"

Russell laid the pen on top of his notebook. "I am very aware of what's going on, Riley. The question is, why are you?"

Did that matter at this point? I had a tendency to step into things I had no business being involved in. But now I was involved, the ache in my thigh was a big indicator of that.

"It's too late for you to reprimand me."

Russell's nostrils flared, sniffing the air. "Were you bit?"

"Someone attacked Riley at Peaceful Acres," Ethan responded.

Concern nestled between Russell's brows. He glanced past me to look at his pack mate. "Who was it?"

"We don't know," I answered for Ethan. "They were using Wolfsbane to mask their scent. Ethan and Michael—" I snapped my jaw shut. Russell's gaze rested on me. "Michael has nothing to do with this."

"I know."

"Then why have you been looking for him?"

"The whole pack knew of the changes our alpha made. I knew Michael's life was in danger."

Maisie set a cup of coffee in front of me, and I wrapped my hands around it, bringing it to my lips. She set one in front of Russell, but he barely acknowledged it. No surprise there.

"Do you know who's behind Sasha's murder, and Eugene's disappearance?"

His tongue flicked out to lick his lips and he gave a small nod.

"Why aren't you arresting him?" I asked.

"It's not that simple." Russell slid his finger through the handle of the cup and scooted it closer. My lips parted as I watched him bring it to his mouth. I never thought I'd ever see him drink

A Deadly Secret

coffee. "I have no evidence to arrest him on. There has been no discussion inside the pack to incriminate him. Even if he orchestrated this, I have to have solid evidence. But he would never see the inside of a jail cell."

"Why not?"

Ethan cleared his throat. "A werewolf in a human jail."

I sighed. They were right. But there had to be something they could do . . . something the wolf pack could do. He wasn't fighting fair. He was having someone else get their hands dirty so his would stay clean and there would be nothing to tie him to the murder of his wife.

He picked up his pad of paper and slid it back into his breast pocket. Setting the hat on top of his head, Russell stood. "Please let the pack handle this. There's no need for you to get hurt . . . any further."

He thanked Maisie for the coffee and showed himself to the door, the paper bag of Wolfsbane nestled under his arm. I winced as I stood. I had no intention of listening to him. I planned on finding something, anything, to tie Manuel Vargas to the murder of his wife and, possibly, Eugene. Someone had to take the fall, and it would be the one responsible.

Maisie brought the grimoire from her room and unlocked it. I suppose if we couldn't use 'human' justice, we could always use supernatural justice. But first, we had to find Eugene, and I prayed he was still alive.

Holding my hands over the first page of the grimoire, I closed my eyes and thought "location spell." I felt a breeze from the pages as they flipped. The grimoire settled on a page with flowery script.

I grabbed a scrap piece of paper as Maisie read the spell out

201

loud. It seemed simple enough: five drops of Forget-Me-Not oil, something from the body of the missing, a quartz pendulum, and a map.

"Ethan, do you think you can find Michael?" I glanced at him. He had taken a seat at the table, watching us. He blinked slowly and pulled his gaze to meet mine.

"Sorry." He stood and walked toward the grimoire. "Michael. Yeah, I should be able to find him."

"Good. If we are going to locate his father, I need something that contains . . ." I glanced back at the book. "DNA, I guess. So, a toothbrush or hairbrush?"

"Got it." He pressed his hand against the small of my back, leaned down, and kissed me. The heat I had felt earlier flooded into my cheeks. His eyes twinkled, a smirk touched his lips. He knew what I was feeling. Could he smell it? Was I giving off a newly acquired pheromone?

Ethan pulled his truck keys from his pocket and laid them on the counter. "You can't be walking around to find the rest of those items." He pressed his lips against the top of my head and then walked out the side door.

"You okay?" Maisie raised an eyebrow.

I pressed my hands to my cheeks to cool them off. "I have no idea."

Something inside the house slammed, followed by a shriek. I spun around, grunting with pain, and looked into the living room. I could hear a rattle—metal hitting metal. Exchanging glances with Maisie, her eyes widened.

"The cage!"

Chapter 38

Maisie and I stared into the cage behind the stairs. She snapped her fingers and the room filled with light. The cage teetered on its base. A little creature, with the now-empty bowl in front of its face, cowered against the back bars. Long, pointy ears peeked over the top of the bowl and equally long toes with sharp nails poked from underneath.

Leaning closer, I squinted, trying to figure out what *it* was. It jumped forward with a loud screech and banged the bowl against the cage. I stumbled backward with a yelp.

"Let me out!" it squeaked, banging the bowl on the bars again.

It couldn't be more than a foot tall, resembling a brown bat, with thin, veiny wings and an upright, pig-like snout. It pressed its nose to the bars, dropping the bowl and grabbing onto the cage to try to shake its way out.

Could this really be what has been following me around? An overgrown bat?

It looked up at me, its mouth drew down in a frown and a tear ran down its cheek. "Please, let me out."

"Oh, God, Riley! It's crying!" Maisie reached for the cage door.

I put my hand on hers. "Wait—what if it's faking?"

Maisie looked at me, her face matching that of the creature's. "I don't think it's faking. It looks terrified."

I picked up the cage. The little creature held on tighter as I brought it to the kitchen table. "I'm going to open the door."

It moved away from the door, picking the bowl up, then held it in front of itself as a shield. Or maybe it planned on using it as a weapon. A tiny mixing bowl probably wouldn't hurt too badly, unless it was used against an ankle.

"Please don't attack us," I begged and opened the door.

"Attack witches?" It moved the bowl to rest on top of its head like a hat, forcing its ears down. "Never hurt witches." It slowly moved from the cage, squinting up at me.

I moved a chair to sit a few feet away. "Have you been following me?"

"I was helping." It gave a big, pointy-toothed smile. Its little chest puffed out in what I could only imagine was a feeling of accomplishment.

"Helping?" Maisie leaned over my shoulder.

"Who sent you?" I asked.

It winced, looking down and rubbing its foot back and forth on the table. "Please don't hurt me."

"We aren't going to hurt you," I said, trying to use my most reassuring voice. "Can you please tell us who sent you?"

"She wants you to be ready." It pulled the bowl over its face to hide.

"Who?" I pressed.

"If she knows you caught me, she'll hurt me!" It looked

204

A Deadly Secret

over the rim of the bowl. A river of tears cascaded down its cheeks as it blinked.

"Okay . . ." I exchanged a glance with Maisie. If it wouldn't tell us who sent it, maybe it would tell us something else. "Can you tell us your name?"

"H—Harold." He lowered the bowl back to his belly. "I can help you with your spell."

Maisie moved a chair to sit in front of him. "How so?"

A large grin spread across its face, forcing its eyes to squint. "I can get the pendulum. I'll get it. Harold is very quiet and very sneaky."

I couldn't argue with that. He put the bowl back on his head and vanished, leaving a light breeze in his wake. The bowl spun haphazardly on the table. Maisie picked it up, looking just as perplexed as I felt. Her brows were scrunched, her lips pursed.

"Who do you think he was talking about?"

Shrugging, I crossed my arms. " I have no idea." Agatha? Maybe Esther? I had no idea who "she" was and why anyone would need us ready. What did we need to be ready for?

Maisie stood, pushing her chair back under the table. "Let's finish getting the supplies." She grabbed Ethan's keys off the counter and held the door open for me.

Grabbing the list, I grunted as I walked down the steps leading out of the kitchen to the driveway. I was going to regret not staying in bed today.

Just a few minutes later, Maisie pulled the truck into an empty spot in front of the flower shop. To say I was grateful for not having to limp down the street, was an understatement. The poultice was helping, but there was still a deep ache in my thigh.

Connie looked up from the counter. She hastily told the person on the other end goodbye and from the look on her face, I wondered what gossip she was spreading. She placed the phone back on the cradle and stood.

"Well." She chuckled, walking around the counter toward Maisie and me. "Isn't this a treat. How can I help you girls?"

"Do you have any forget-me-nots?"

"It's not really their season." Connie tapped a finger to her pursed lips, then raised her arms in a big shrug. "But that's never stopped me before."

I pulled the list out of my pocket, catching Connie's attention. She held her hand out and I gave it to her. Putting it up close to her face, she scrunched her brows and then held it further away. "Oil of forget-me-nots?" She glanced at us over the paper. "What exactly are you two up to?"

Shuffling my feet, I glanced at Maisie.

Connie flicked her eyes to the ceiling. "All right, don't tell me."

She motioned for us to follow before disappearing into the back room. By the time we caught up, she was standing in front of a large, wooden cabinet. It had dozens of drawers with little white-and-bronze knobs. Small labels had been added above each one, sectioning the alphabet all the way to the bottom right drawer.

She pulled open one drawer and picked through a few glass jars, dropping them arbitrarily. "Ah!" She held one up and turned to us, a large grin on her face.

"Will this be enough?"

I took the amber-colored jar by the rubber dropper attached to the top and held it sideways. The liquid inside slid back and forth like molasses, a few forget-me-nots attached themselves to the side of the glass. "It should be. Thank you."

"I think it's time you two start gathering supplies every witch should have," Connie mentioned as we walked back into the shop.

"I wouldn't even know where to begin. Agatha is so preoccupied these days."

Connie laughed. "Oh, that's nothing new. She's always been like that. Now, your mother was more—" Connie stopped, pressing a hand over her mouth. "Oh, I'm sorry. I shouldn't have brought her up."

"No, it's okay." I had a feeling the people in Wildewood knew more about our mother than they let on. She had lived here her whole life. Everyone was so scared to talk about her. It wasn't as if she could hurt us anymore. She had given us up and was now gone. Why hide what she was?

"I'd be happy to help you two. One of these days when you aren't running around doing"—she fluttered her hands in front of her—"whatever it is you two do."

"We'd really appreciate that." I thanked her again and we left the store.

"What's next?" Maisie looked over my arm at the list as I crossed off the Forget-Me-Not oil. "A map. Do people even sell those anymore now that everyone has a phone?" She snorted and mumbled, "Well, everyone except for us."

Looking around town, I wondered where we could find a map. The Stop and Shop wasn't too far away, but I had never seen a map there only the latest tabloids. "There's that little

gas station right before the bridge." I shoved the list back in
my pocket as I climbed into Ethan's truck. After buckling, I
looked up and saw Bean bounding down the sidewalk toward
us.

Maisie opened her door. Bean jumped onto her lap then
into the back. She reversed out of the parking spot and did,
what I'm certain, was an illegal U-turn to head toward the
main road that led out of Wildewood.

The gas station was one of those old, two-pump stations
that looked like it came out of a movie from the 1960s. The
convenience store was small and rounded on one side, the
white paint faded from years in the sun. The other side of the
building was a quick oil change shop but was no longer in use.
I leaned toward Maisie to see the gas gauge and figured we
should fuel up the truck so Ethan didn't have to later.

Pulling next to a pump, I gave Maisie some cash and she
hurried inside to pay and hopefully grab a map. I placed the
nozzle into the gas tank and leaned against the cold metal of
the truck. A dark SUV pulled into the station lot. It turned
toward the pump beside the truck with Manuel Vargas in the
driver seat.

Ducking to the other side of the truck, I peeked through
the window and watched him exit his vehicle. He started to
pump his gas when his phone rang. While he leaned across the
seat to grab it, I looked toward the gas station, hoping Maisie
wasn't done yet.

The conversation with the person on his phone was
hushed. His neck grew red as he strained his words, and then
he raised his voice, "Take care of it!"

I pressed a hand over my mouth, ducking down further.

"This is your mess, clean it up." His door slammed.

I peeked back through the window. Though his windows had a slight tint, I could see the anger on his face. Deep wrinkles penetrated his forehead as he yelled a chain of curse words that would make anyone blush before starting his car up. He pulled out of the small parking lot and I walked as fast as I could to the building. Looking over my shoulder at his vehicle speeding away, I wondered who the hell he had been talking to. I turned back around and ran into Maisie as she stepped out of the door. A bottle of water fell out of her hand and started to roll across the asphalt. Scooping it up, I grabbed her wrist and pulled her to the truck.

"Riley!" she yelped.

Ignoring the pain in my thigh, I slid into the driver seat and motioned for her to hurry. As soon as her door closed, I pressed on the gas. The truck roared to life and the tires squealed as we sped out of the parking lot.

"What happened?" She looked behind her at Bean, who was not excited about my driving. "I was only gone for a few minutes." She grabbed the handle above her.

"Vargas. He was on the phone, telling someone to 'clean up the mess.' I think we've run out of time."

Maisie cursed under her breath.

"I need you to trust me, but I think Jessica Freki is working with him." She had been arguing with Sasha at the Christmas party, leaving shortly after Sasha ran into the bathroom. It's possible she had gone that way without me noticing. She had the Wolfsbane perfume. And she was conveniently 'out sick' right after I was attacked. "We have to stop her."

I sped through Wildewood, only slowing as we rounded the square. I had been to Jessica Freki's house only one time. Tessa had been dropping off a few things from Odds 'n' Ends and I happened to be with her. I knew it was close to the bed and breakfast Maisie had lived in for months before she moved in with me. I hoped she was still there and that we had a chance to stop her.

Chapter 39

Through the trees, the setting sun on the horizon created a deep orange, the clouds above were dark blue and red. Driving faster than the speed limit allowed, we finally reached Jessica's street. I slowed, seeing her house. Pulling over a few houses before hers, I let the truck idle as it dawned on me that we might be heading into a dangerous situation. I couldn't just walk into Jessica's without a plan.

She had to be the person behind all of this. Even if I didn't understand what she was gaining from it. It was possible Vargas was forcing her through the use of Wolfsbane. I knew he was pulling the strings . . . I just wasn't sure who was pulling his.

"What are we doing?" Maisie unbuckled her seatbelt to twist in her seat to face me.

"I'm thinking." I closed my eyes and laid my head against the worn-out steering wheel.

Sophia said Jessica wasn't feeling well. If I had thought this through, instead of running toward danger like an idiot, I could've come up with a plan. I could've picked up some soup and used that as an in. I looked around the floorboards and

211

spotted a to-go bag from Mikes. Grabbing it, I opened it and gagged at the rancid smell within. It would have to do.

If nothing else, the smell might incapacitate her and give us an advantage.

"Okay. Here's the plan," I climbed out and looked at Maisie over the hood of the truck. "We are just here to check on her, to see if she's okay."

"And if she doesn't welcome us with open arms?"

Biting my bottom lip, I took in a deep breath. "Then we wing it." We're witches, for crying out loud. We could handle a dog. A very large, ferocious, wild dog.

My pace slowed as I walked up the path to Jessica's front door, a knot forming in the pit of my stomach. The door was cracked open, the frame split as if it had been forced. Making as little noise as I could, I held my breath and pushed the door further open with the sleeve of my sweatshirt.

We walked into a well-lit house, but it was quiet. Too quiet. Maisie touched my arm. She put one finger to her mouth and another to her ear, tilting her head. I stilled my breathing and listened. I heard a soft gasp, someone struggling for breath. The bag slipped from my fingers and I ran toward the whimpering.

Bounding up the stairs as fast as I could, I poked my head into the only open door and saw Jessica. She was lying on her bedroom floor, still in her pajamas. One of her slippers had been knocked off, the other just barely hanging onto her toes. I could barely make out the rise and fall of her chest but I could hear her unsteady breathing. Dropping to my knees, I hissed from a sharp pain radiating through my leg. I grabbed her hand and her eyes slowly rolled to look at me.

"Jessica."

Foam dripped from the side of her mouth. She had been poisoned. Her lips moved, barely. Her fingers tightened on my hand just enough to notice. I leaned closer, trying to hear what she whispered, but without being able to breathe, her voice was so soft I struggled to make it out.

"Stop." She took a breath. "Sophia."

Her grip loosened and her hand slipped from mine. "No, no! Jessica!" I patted her cheek but her eyes rolled into the back of her head. Dammit! I wasn't expecting this. If I had thought Jessica was in danger, I would've brought the tincture Connie had given me. "Please wake up!" I shook her.

Maisie walked into the room and I turned my head to look at her, tears running down my cheek. "Call Russell."

I watched as Jessica's breathing slowed, and repeated what she said over and over again in my head: Stop Sophia. Was the sheriff's niece behind all of this? Were they working together? I bumped into her dresser, the contents knocking over and I noticed the perfume from her boutique in its pretty, chiseled glass bottle. She didn't have a cold. It had been making her sick for days, but someone had come to finish the job. Had Manuel been talking to Sophia on the phone?

I picked up the empty bottle, the atomizer had been yanked off and was lying beside it. Maisie yelled up the steps for me to come on. She met me in the foyer. "We have to go." She pulled me from the house, grabbing the rancid to-go bag off the floor. "Russell's coming, but he warned us we should leave."

Giving Maisie the keys, I walked in a daze back to the truck, this time climbing into the passenger seat. She drove past Jessica's and made a U-turn. Pulling the truck over on the neighboring street, we could still see the house.

"Did she say anything?" Maisie finally broke the silence as we waited.

"Stop Sophia."

"Vargas' niece?" Maisie jerked her head toward me. "She murdered her own aunt?"

And Jessica. And probably Eugene. She was trying to win the role of alpha for her uncle by any means necessary and these three got in the way. I stared at Jessica's house. It felt as if I had been holding my breath until I heard the sound of a siren. A patrol car turned onto the street, followed by an ambulance.

Maybe they had come in time, but I doubted it. I was certain Jessica had lost the battle the moment her hand slipped from mine. Tears stung my eyes and I quickly wiped them away. Officer Russell ran into the house and, a moment later, back out to the EMS carrying a stretcher.

Sophia had fooled us. She had fooled me.

Was this what Manuel Vargas wanted? When he told her to clean up her mess, was this what he intended? He lost his wife. Jessica was murdered. All for what? Peaceful Acres? What could be so important about that land?

I glanced at Maisie, who was staring intently at Jessica's. She wiped a tear from her eye. I could never imagine doing anything that would cost her life. How could he sacrifice his wife? I would do anything to keep Maisie safe. Anything.

The EMS came out of Jessica's house with a black body bag strapped to the stretcher. My body shuttered and I leaned back against the seat, letting out a deep sigh. They had been too late.

"Dammit!" I slapped the dashboard. I leaned down, resting my head on my knees, trying to breathe away the panic swarming me.

"Let's go home," Maisie whispered as she put the truck in drive, taking a longer way around, so we didn't have to go past Jessica's.

There was nothing else we could do here. Officer Russell would take care of it, and probably hide the link to the sheriff. The law was not on our side this time, because the big guy in charge was the problem.

Chapter 40

Ethan and Michael were waiting for us as we pulled into the driveway. They sat on the concrete steps that led into the kitchen under the carport. Ethan stood when the truck engine turned off. He walked to the truck and pulled my door open. His bright-blue eyes searched my face.

"What's wrong?"

I couldn't keep how distraught I was from him. A tear slid down my cheek. Ethan wrapped his hands around my waist and helped me out and onto the driveway. I had moved too fast, too abruptly at Jessica's. I could feel my pulse under the bandage. With the back of my hand, I wiped away a stray tear. "Jessica Freki is dead."

Michael's lips parted. He and Ethan exchanged a worried look. "How?"

"Sophia poisoned her." I limped past them into the kitchen.

Maisie laid the map she'd found at the gas station on the table, opening it to expose all of Wildewood. On the top left corner, it read "Adventure in Wildewood!" There wasn't much to do outside of shopping and hiking, but little did the creators of the map know, Wildewood would become more interesting than just visiting the waterfalls.

I placed the glass jar of Forget-Me-Not oil beside the map, taking a glance at Michael. "Did you find anything of your father's?"

He handed me a tissue covered in blood. Wrinkling my nose, I pinched the only clean spot and took it. "Dad had a nose bleed last week."

Maisie brought one of my larger, chrome mixing bowls over and placed it beside the map. We almost had everything we needed; the bloody tissue, a match from the junk drawer near the sink, and the Forget-Me-Not oil.

"All that's missing is the pendu—" I stopped at the sound of something skittering across the floor.

Harold appeared on the table, grinning from ear to pointy ear. He held up a pendulum. "I told you Harold knew where one was."

"What the hell is that?" Ethan asked, putting a hand on my shoulder. I could feel him trying to move me backward, but I wouldn't budge.

Harold tucked his head into his shoulders, his grin turning into a frown.

"It's a hobgoblin." I shrugged Ethan's hand off and looked at both men. "Be nice."

I took the pendulum. It was more of a smokey quartz, not completely clear but hopefully, that didn't matter. "Where did you get this from?" I asked.

"The same place your book was." He grabbed his ears and pulled them down over his eyes. "Don't be mad."

"I'm not mad," I reassured him. Though, I couldn't say the same for the mayor. "Thank you, Harold."

Maisie opened the grimoire to the location spell. She read the directions out loud. Placing the bloody tissue into the bowl, I then dropped in exactly five drops of the oil. As it was absorbed by the tissue, I held the match against the box, ready to strike.

"What is lost, is now found," Maisie recited in Latin.

I struck the match against the box then dropped it into the bowl.

A plume of smoke rose as the fire quickly consumed the items. Picking up the pendulum, I held it over the map. Together we repeated the spell. The smokey-colored stone began to swing back and forth in long strides.

I could feel the heat radiating off Ethan's body as he stood behind me. Bean jumped onto the table and Harold took a few timid steps backward until Bean laid down. His eyes moved back and forth, watching the pendulum. The swings became shorter until it moved in a tight circle. It felt heavier than before.

A knock came at the door, causing me to jump and lose hold of the metal chain attached to the pendulum. The knocking became more frantic. Ethan rushed into the hallway, and I could hear Jennifer's voice.

"Is Michael here?" She brushed past her brother and into the kitchen, still wearing her Just Treats apron.

Her eyes widened as she looked at the table, probably just as unsure about Harold as the rest of us had been. I watched as her gaze swooped from him to the slightly smoking bowl in front of me and then to Michael.

"We have to go."

Michael's shoulders tensed. "What's going on?"

"Eugene—" She licked her lips. "Vargas is challenging him."

Michael pushed away from the island. "He's alive." He let out a sigh of relief.

Jennifer motioned for him to follow. "Hurry." She looked at me for a second before walking out of view.

Without saying goodbye, Ethan and Michael ran after her. I followed to the door and watched them climb into her small, dark-blue sedan. My stomach started to knot. There was no way Eugene was in any shape to fight Vargas, even as a wolf. If I was right, he had been poisoned just enough to subdue him and probably slowly brought to the brink of death the way Jessica had been.

I knew this wasn't our business, we weren't werewolves, but when did I ever listen?

I shut the front door and met Maisie in the hallway. "We have to follow them."

She pulled her bottom lip between her teeth. "I don't think that's a good idea."

"Eugene is in trouble!" I pleaded.

"But they're . . ." Maisie followed on my heels as I walked back to the table. "The last time you were around a wolf, you almost died."

Running my hand through my hair, I looked at her over my shoulder. "Eugene *will* die. We have the antidote he needs."

Kicking myself, I realized I should've stopped them before they left but it was too late now. The car was gone. I didn't even know where they were going. I closed my eyes and took in a deep breath. Opening them, I saw the pendulum standing straight up, its point digging into the map. I pulled it away, seeing an indention in Peaceful Acres. He had been there all along. No doubt

Sophia had used Wolfsbane to mask his scent, that's probably why the boys hadn't been able to find him.

Ethan's truck was still in the driveway, but we needed to get to him fast, and preferably undetected. I held my hand out, the broom beside the trash can shaking to life. It slammed into my palm. "If you want to stay, I understand."

Masie's jaw clenched and then she shook her head. "No. There's no way in hell I'm letting you go alone."

Chapter 41

For once, Maisie didn't complain about my mode of transportation. She grabbed her jacket and headed toward the back door. "Come on, let's go."

I followed her, pulling my own jacket over the already-thick WPD sweatshirt. while trying to hold on to the broom. Harold was on my heels, his feet making a clicking sound on the hardwood. I turned to him. "Harold. I think you should wait here."

As I turned back around, Agatha materialized in front of the door, arms crossed over her chest. She looked down at the hobgoblin, causing Harold to scream and grab at my leg to hide. Agatha narrowed her eyes and pointed. "Where did you find that?"

"He found us." I stepped aside, so she could see him, but he fell to the ground, still holding onto my pants and I ended up dragging him. Bean crept into the hallway; his tail swished as he observed us. Or maybe he thought Harold was a snack.

"Someone let you out." Agatha kneeled down. Her form flickered slightly as she became more translucent.

Harold clutched at my leg, his little nails digging into my skin.

"Harold. Come here. I'm not going to hurt you." When he didn't budge, she sighed. "It's me, Agatha."

"But you're . . ." he tugged on my pants, pushing his face between my legs to look at her. I grabbed the waist of the baggy sweatpants, afraid he was going to pull them down.

"Dead, yes. But I'm back." She stood, her hips tilted to one side, her arms out.

Harold's hold on me loosened. He walked around my feet, craning his neck to look up at her. "Wildewoods are so tricky." He followed her back into the kitchen. "They never seem to stay dead."

"Be nice to him." I pointed at her. "We'll be back."

I hoped we'd be back, at least. I felt the glass bottle in my pocket as it hit against my thigh, realizing I had no idea how I'd be able to get close enough to Eugene without putting myself in danger. But at this point, I didn't have enough time to make another plan.

"Go with them," Agatha hissed, swiping her hand in the air from Bean to us.

Bean jumped to his feet. He padded toward us, out the door, and onto the back porch. Maisie and I got ourselves situated on the broom, though, with two people on one broom, it was never truly comfortable. He jumped into my arms and I zipped my jacket around his little body with only his head poking out.

"*Subvolare!*" I yelled, wrapping my hands around the handle.

The broom rose slowly, the toes of my boots scraping the ground. I heard Maisie whisper and we jutted into the night sky so fast I almost lost control. The wind blew the hood off my head as we sped toward the edge of town.

The moon was already rising, the sun having set at least an hour before. It was large and full. If pop culture was accurate, this was a dangerous time to be around a group of werewolves. But Eugene was more important at this moment. I only wished I knew more spells I could use to keep us safe.

We veered away from the bridge, careful to stay within the town limits, otherwise, we'd be powerless, and there was nothing below to cushion our fall. Flying over the clearing at the entrance of Peaceful Acres, we hovered high above the Christmas tree farm. I spotted Jennifer's car parked with a half-dozen other cars in the gravel parking lot.

"I don't know where to go," I called over my shoulder.

The location spell had brought us this far, but Peaceful Acres was large. Maisie pointed toward the ground below us. The light from the moon exposed a hefty shape running through the trees. I pulled us up further and followed the creature.

We neared a smaller clearing. Wolves and humans alike moved in the empty space. A large cabin sat tucked in the trees. We inched closer to the ground behind it. Mostly shielded from sight, it was the safest place I could think of to land.

My feet touched the soft ground. Maisie slid off the broom, falling backward. She jumped to her feet as I unzipped my jacket to free Bean. Leaving the broom on the ground, I crouched underneath a window and peeked over the frame into a small bedroom. Maisie pressed her body against the smooth logs and peered into another. She looked at me, shaking her head.

It would've been too easy had Eugene been alone in the cabin. He had to be around here somewhere. I just didn't know how to find him without revealing our arrival to the others. I kicked myself, wishing I had spritzed us with that awful perfume to mask our scent. I heard a noise inside the cabin and sucked in a breath, creeping to the window Maisie stood beside.

I stopped moving but the sound of leaves crunching continued. Something was close. I looked over my shoulder and a tall figure moved in the shadows. I grabbed at Maisie, adrenaline rushing through me, my heart rate quickened and I held my hand out, a spell at the tip of my tongue.

"It's me." Ethan moved out of the shadows, holding his palms up. He placed a finger over his mouth. "You shouldn't be here," he whispered, grabbing my elbow and pulling me toward the tree line.

"There's no way Eugene can fight Vargas." I drew the glass bottle from my pocket.

"Where is he?" Maisie piped in.

A howl broke through the silence, Ethan's grip tightened around my arm, his fingers digging in. I stiffened, turning around to face the cabin. Ethan spun me back around, pulling me further. I looked into his golden eyes, the blue only a tiny sliver.

"Go home." He brushed his hand against my jaw, his lips thin with worry. "Please, go home." His hands dropped to his side and he ran toward the front of the cabin.

Maisie's finger interlocked with mine. I glanced at her and she nodded. "Let's go."

But we didn't go back to the broom. We moved through the darkness, pressed against the cabin until we reached the edge. There were fewer humans now, more wolves. They paced the tree line and I knew at any moment one of them would spot us.

The front door of the cabin opened, light spilling onto the

dark lawn. Eugene stumbled from the doorway, falling to his hands and knees. Vargas stomped toward him, announcing to the wolves that he was challenging the current alpha. The hair on the back of my neck stood at the sound of snarls and snapping jaws in response.

This wasn't a fair fight.

Eugene pushed himself up onto his knees. He held his chin up and looked at the man before him. Gritting my teeth, I stopped myself from going to him, from screaming for this to stop.

Something touched my leg and I slapped a hand over my mouth. Looking at the ground, Beans bright-yellow eyes locked onto mine. I knew that look. I reached to grab him but he ran toward Eugene.

Vargas jerked his head toward us. I screamed through my hand. Bean ran past the men, catching their attention, and I ran after him. This was a terrible idea. A stupid idea. He was going to get himself killed, and probably us too.

I had no idea how many wolves were on either side of this challenge. For all we knew, only Ethan, Michael, and Jennifer were standing on Eugene's side. I dug my heels into the ground as Vargas threw his head back and howled. His body began to change in a ripple of muscle under his skin, the same as Ethan's had.

I slid to the ground, crying out from the pain in my thigh. Stomach acid rose in my throat and I forced myself to swallow it. I could cry about my thigh later. I laid my hand on Eugene's bloodied arm and he blinked at me.

"Riley . . ." his voice was hoarse. His eyes could barely focus. The skin on his face was blue and purple, one eye blackened and

225

half shut from the swelling. They beat him too? Was poisoning him not enough? I touched his cheek and he winced.

Scrambling to get the jar out of my pocket, I looked at Vargas. He was almost fully changed. His arms no longer looked like a man's, and a snout began to form. I didn't have more than a few seconds.

"Please, trust me," I begged Eugene and unscrewed the lid. Realizing Connie didn't give me any instructions, I threw the dropper to the side and pressed the opening to his busted lip, and he opened his mouth.

His throat moved vigorously. I dropped the empty jar, it rolled down the hill toward Vargas. Eugene gagged. Please do not throw it up. I had no idea what it was made of and by Eugene's reaction, it mustn't taste great. I scooted away as Eugene fell forward onto his hands. His coughs were loud and painful. His arms gave out, he hit the ground with a loud thud and went still.

A cry escaped me, and I stared at his lifeless body. Had I been too late?

Movement in front of me caught my attention. Sophia barreled toward us, her body changing as she ran. Fur broke out over her legs, her arms. Her clothing ripped as more fur exploded from her skin to cover her chest. It ran up her neck, her face becoming elongated as it transformed into a snout.

Sophia launched herself at us. I screamed, covering my head with my arms. There was no time for me to move out of the way. Another scream came from behind me. I looked past my arms to see Sophia being tossed backward mid-jump. Turning around, Maisie stood with her palms held out in front of her.

Her chest rose and fell rapidly as she lowered her arms to her side. She looked at me, her eyes wide. Her nostrils flared, tears streaming down her cheeks. Pushing myself up from the ground, I backed up toward her, waiting for Sophia to get up.

The wolf laid sprawled out, her mouth hanging open and her long, pink tongue dangling. She didn't budge. I couldn't see her chest moving. I glanced at Maisie. She raised her hands to cover her mouth, her brows pulled together.

A growl rang out and I watched as Eugene pushed himself up from the ground. The antidote must've worked! He lifted his head, rolling his shoulders back, his chest puffing out. Eugene glanced at us. "It's time you two go."

He turned his attention to Vargas who subsequently backed up, his tail between his legs at the realization his plan had failed. Eugene began to shift into a large, black wolf. His form towered over Vargas'. I then understood Sasha's fear of her husband challenging the alpha. He was no match for the alpha.

Eugen took one last look at us, giving a slight nod before turning back to his foe. I grabbed Maisie's hand and pulled her behind the cabin to the broom where Bean was waiting for us. I grabbed him. The howls of the wolves caused goosebumps to rise on my skin. My stomach turned as we listened to what could only be the tearing of flesh, and I knew we had to leave now. Right now.

Chapter 42

Maisie ran inside the house. She had been silent the whole ride home. Her head buried into my shoulder, wetting my jacket with her tears. I didn't want to say anything, or rather, I didn't know what to say.

She had killed Sophia.

My arms dangled heavily; my shoulders sagged. The broom slipped from my grasp, the snow silencing its fall. I choked back a cry, turning away from the open door. What had I done?

This was all my fault.

If I hadn't insisted we go to Peaceful Acres, this would've never happened. My stomach turned and I leaned over the porch railing, emptying its contents. I would've done anything to protect her, and yet she followed me into a situation we should've never been involved in.

Running the back of my hand over my mouth, I could barely see through my tears. I looked down at the broom. My fingers tingled, electricity violently pulsing through my veins. I raised my hand into the air, the broom following, and threw the broom toward the tree in the back.

The broom exploded into wooden shavings as it hit the trunk. Why was it so difficult for me to use my magic? Why was it so easy for Maisie?

I ran down the steps, ignoring the growing pain in my leg, and fell to my knees. Pounding my hands on the frozen ground, I screamed. The bushes beside the house unearthed in a burst of dirt and snow.

"Riley!" Agatha called from behind me.

My scream turned into a silent sob and I slumped over. My fists opened; my hands red from the cold. The electricity I felt fizzled away as if the snow had cooled it.

"What happened? Maisie won't come out of her room and you—you're tearing up the landscaping," Agatha asked, hovering in front of me.

I looked up at her, sniffling. "Maisie used her magic to kill."

Agatha motioned for me to stand. She placed her hand on my arm, her jaw tightening, and for a second I felt the weight of it. I pushed myself up, knowing she couldn't help me and walked back up the porch steps then into the house.

"Do you know what spell she used?" her voice was low. She waved her hand and the back door closed.

I shook my head. My throat felt as if it were closing, and all I could do was shake my head.

Agatha touched my arm again. I knew it took every ounce of energy for her to truly touch me. I looked into her eyes. She brushed her other hand over my head, barely moving a piece of hair back. "She'll be okay."

Even though she was dead, the lines on her forehead deepened. She didn't believe a word she said, and neither did I.

We were cursed. One of us would go mad with power. I

worried now more than ever that Maisie would be the one to lose her sanity as the power of our magic consumed her. And it was all my fault. I would do anything to take back that moment, to find an alternative. But unfortunately, I was certain I couldn't turn back the hand of time. We would have to deal with whatever came our way, and I would be right beside her.

I kicked my boots off at the bottom of the stairs. It took longer to reach the loft; my thigh burned and I was certain I had damaged the stitches. Pulling my wet clothes off, I threw them into the hamper and put on a pair of drawstring, black pajama pants and a T-shirt of Ethan's.

I walked back down the stairs, my body growing tired with every step I took. Outside of Maisie's room, I listened to her quiet sobs. Pushing the door open, my chest tightened seeing her small frame curled in a ball on top of the comforter. Her shoulders bobbed as she cried into the pillow she held against her.

I crawled beside her, my arm going around her shoulders, and whispered, "I'm so sorry."

Chapter 43

I woke to Ethan gently shaking my shoulder. Maisie was quiet, her breathing steady as she slept. Slipping off her bed, I followed him into the kitchen and gasped as I turned on the light. He was bruised and bloody.

Grabbing a clean washcloth from the bathroom, I dampened it and pulled him to the couch. Pressing it against a deep cut on Ethan's cheek, I could barely wrap my mind around the blood, gashes, and bites covering his body. Had they transferred from his wolf form to his human one? Ethan winced. He wrapped his fingers around my wrist and pulled my hand away.

"I promise, I'll be fine." He took the cloth from my fingers.

"You look terrible."

His eyes sparkled, his lips turning up into a smile but the cut stopped him. "I promise. I heal quickly."

"What happened after I left last night?" I took the washcloth back and proceeded to deal with a bloody cut on his arm.

Ethan sighed, leaning back against the couch. He lowered his head, staring at his fingers in his lap. "Pack issues."

A bubble of anger welled up inside of me. I tossed the

washcloth beside him. "Dammit, Ethan. Stop trying to hide things from me."

Ethan took a deep breath, wincing as he ran his fingers through his hair. "Okay. You're right."

"Is Vargas still alive?"

"Yes." His head bobbed in a slow nod.

"How?" I questioned, certain Eugene would have killed him after what he had done.

"He conceded."

There was a dark part of me that wished he was dead, but I felt relief knowing Eugene had shown mercy. Even though Sophia had been responsible for the death of his wife, Jessica, and had put Eugene in a weakened state, Vargas hadn't stopped her. But that's because she had been doing his bidding.

"What is going to happen to him now?" I asked.

"He has to leave the pack."

"That's it?" That's pack justice? He gets to walk free after orchestrating a takeover that went against not only pack policy, but human laws? Sophia may have been the one with blood on her hands, but Vargas was far from innocent.

"No, that's not it," Ethan snapped.

A scowl spread across my face. "Then what? Where is he?"

Ethan brushed a strand of hair from my cheek. He took a deep breath. "I'm struggling to open up to you." He gave a weak smile. "I've only ever talked to other pack members about these things."

My chest tightened, and I let out a shaky breath. This was the first time I felt Ethan was truly trying to let me in. I didn't want to say anything that would cause him to slam the door shut again.

"There's a place in Twin Falls . . ." He licked his busted lip. "A jail, so to speak, for supernaturals."

My voice was a whisper, "Is that where he is?"

Ethan nodded. "He can never see the inside of a human jail. It would be too dangerous. Humans can never know we exist."

I rubbed his forearm, a gentle way to thank him for opening up. His forehead creased; he pinched the bridge of his nose. Looking at me, the gold in his eyes was not as prominent anymore.

"I suppose there's no reason to keep anything from you now." He took my hand and brushed his lips over my knuckles.

"Will you tell me about Peaceful Acres? I don't understand why that land is so important."

I understood that the wolf pack used the land, that it passed from alpha to alpha. I understood that Eugene changed that, but not why it would cause Vargas to let his wife be murdered.

"I know why."

I looked behind me to see Harold standing between the kitchen and living room. He turned the small, chrome-colored bowl in his hands as he fidgeted, his right foot stroked the floor and he cast his eyes down.

Facing him, I leaned down, my elbows on my thigh. "Harold? You know why the land is important?"

Agatha appeared behind him. Harold made a mousy shriek, throwing the bowl into the air. He ran toward me and hid behind my back. His little, sharp nails dug into my skin as he grabbed a hold of my shirt. If he kept hanging around, I was going to have to clip those babies. Agatha rolled her eyes. She crossed her arms with her hip cocked.

I glared at her. She'd done that on purpose. Harold was

skittish and she knew it. I pulled him to stand in front of me. "Tell me what you know."

Agatha cleared her throat and Harold pulled his large, pointy ears over his eyes.

Maisie opened her bedroom door and took a step out. "What's going on?" Her hair was matted, her eyes swollen. She still wore the clothes from the night before.

"Harold was just about to tell us why Peaceful Acres was worth killing over."

Maisie walked past Agatha and lowered to her knees in front of the coffee table. "Go on."

"I can show you." He peeked through his ears, finally letting them go, and they sprang back up on the top of his head.

"Show us what?" Maisie asked, laying her hand on the table near him.

"Harold," Agatha warned.

Maisie narrowed her eyes at Agatha, who then threw her hands in the air. She turned back to Harold with a sweet smile tugging on her lips. He held up his finger and disappeared in a streak of black. Within seconds, he returned, holding the picture of Maisie and me with our mother. He laid it in front of us and poked the door in the photo.

"What does this have to do with Peaceful Acres?" I asked.

"The Wildewood mansion," Harold squeaked.

Ethan grabbed the photo, taking a long look at it as he walked into the kitchen. "Supposedly the Wildewood Mansion is on the land. I thought it was just lore."

"Not supposedly," Agatha mumbled.

"What's the Wildewood Mansion?" I followed him.

"Your ancestral home." Agatha floated to sit on the counter.

I looked back at Harold. "Can you take us to it?" I grabbed my jacket, not waiting for a reply, and tossed Maisie hers. Ethan stood in front of the door, blocking my exit.

"Riley, I don't know if that's a good idea. I grew up hearing bad stories about that house."

Maisie had Harold in her arms. "What? Like it's haunted?" She glanced at Agatha.

Ethan's shoulders slumped and he pulled his keys out of his pocket, gripping them tightly as if he were unsure of what to do. He looked past me, and I followed his gaze to Agatha. Great. My boyfriend and dead aunt were in cahoots with one another. At this point, if they wouldn't get out of my way, I would be forced to use magic on them. She would be back in her hat, and he would be stuck to the floor.

Agatha nodded with an exasperated sigh.

"Lead the way, little guy." Ethan opened the door and, before he could change his mind, I stepped outside.

Chapter 44

We loaded into Ethan's truck. Harold sat on the dash-board, trying his best to give directions. He didn't know any street names; he could only tell us to go toward the Falls. The double waterfalls separated our town from Twin Falls, and I hadn't been near them since Leah Crane died by plunging to her death.

This was not the entrance to Peaceful Acres we had gone to previously. That one was right before the bridge that led out of town. But I had to trust Harold and hope he knew how to get to this "Wildewood Mansion" that no one wanted us to know about.

When we got to the top of the Falls, the truck idled in the parking lot. There was nowhere for us to go. Harold stood, squishing his nose to the windshield, his hot breath fogging the glass, and pointed to the tree line.

"We can't drive through trees, Harold," I explained.

He let out a heavy sigh then disappeared. The sun was waking up, a sliver of light on the horizon. I saw the tree line ripple and a paved driveway appeared. Harold once again sat on the dashboard. "All fixed."

Ethan glanced at me.

I shrugged. My curiosity was piqued. It seemed magic had been hiding this from view. But was it Wildewood magic? Ours didn't work at the Falls. I needed to get my hands on a map that showed the true boundary of Wildewood. Ethan pressed on the gas and we drove down a rather steep, winding drive around the Falls until we reached flat land. A large wrought-iron gate appeared in front of us. Two Ws formed in the middle.

"Harold?" I leaned forward.

"Wildewood." He scrambled off the dashboard to hide in my coat.

"We're still in Wildewood?" I opened my coat to look at him.

"Yes." He shook his head and pulled the fabric back over himself.

"We can't get through." Ethan glanced at the bulge at my side. If we were still in Wildewood, Maisie and I could easily unlock the gate.

Unbuckling my seat belt, I grabbed the door handle. Harold disappeared before I could open it and the gate creaked, sounding rusted and needing oil. I wondered how long it'd been since the last time it was opened. Harold reappeared under my jacket as the truck crept through the entrance.

"Oh my God." Maisie gawked from the backseat.

A large, two-story Victorian mansion sat at least a half-mile beyond the gate. Stunning and foreboding, it loomed over us the closer we got. A tower protruded from the right corner of the second floor. A dozen tall windows perfectly spaced out on the top floor gave clues to how many rooms must be inside. Large columns connected the overhang to the porch that wrapped the house.

"Are we in Peaceful Acres?" I whispered.

Harold nodded.

I looked at Ethan. "Was the pack fighting over this place?"

"You'd have to ask Eugene. Believe it or not, there are some things I just don't know."

Ethan parked the truck in the circular driveway in front of the large, double-door entry. I climbed out with Harold huddled on my shoulder, using my hair as a hiding spot.

"We don't go inside," Harold warned, pulling my hair.

"Ow!" I removed my hair from his hands. "Okay. Where do we go?"

He pointed to the side of the mansion. "It's in the back."

We moved through the overgrown brush. The hairs on the back of my neck stood as we walked past the side of the mansion, feeling as if someone was watching us. Harold jumped off my shoulder and ran toward a large, domed building.

I could barely hear him tell us, "Here. In here!"

As we neared the building, I realized it was a greenhouse. Harold jumped and grabbed the doorknob, but it was locked. Maisie snapped her fingers. There was a soft click then the door swung open with Harold still attached to it. I followed behind her as she stepped inside. Maisie cupped her hand, and an orb of light danced on her palm as it drove away some of the darkness. The smell of warm soil and moss wrapped around me. For a place that was abandoned, the greenhouse had been cared for greatly. I looked around in awe at the number of plants growing inside.

"Here." Harold jumped up and down in front of a knee-high wooden border in the back. As we drew closer, I gasped. At least a dozen tall plants with hooded, purple petals.

"Wolfsbane," I said in a hushed tone, letting out my breath.

This was where Sophia got the Wolfsbane. Someone had been growing it up here, out of sight. But who? It could only be someone who knew how to find the mansion, who could see past the magic concealing it.

I kneeled in front of Harold. "Who takes care of these plants?"

A shadow moved outside the building. I grabbed Harold, holding him close to my chest as I stood. We weren't alone. Harold pulled the side of my jacket over him. He was shaking, whimpering. Maisie turned around, as the shadowy figure grew in size. Harold shrieked, large crocodile tears pouring from his big, brown eyes.

Whatever was on the other side of the building, two witches and a werewolf could handle. But the creature in my arms needed to get as far away as possible. If only my legs didn't feel glued to the floor. I looked around and couldn't see the shadow, but it *had* been there. Someone had been outside.

Ethan placed his hand on my arm and pulled me toward the door. "We need to get out of here before he drowns in his tears. I don't think this place is safe."

Maisie stayed behind us, her hands ready to wipe the floor with whatever came our way. I pressed Harold close and ran to the truck. I threw open the door and climbed in. Ethan and Maisie jumped in seconds later. With doors locked, the truck roared to life and we sped back toward the Falls. I pulled Harold away from my body. He was clutching at my shirt, tears and snot mixing, running down his face.

"Harold. Who grows those plants?"

He used my shirt to wipe his face then shook his head. Gross, I groaned to myself. I ran my fingers between his ears, shushing him. He would tell me, but we needed to get out of here. He needed to feel safe before he told what I imagined was a terrible secret.

I looked at Ethan, a deep dread setting in as his jaw tensed. I glanced at Maisie over my shoulder. She was turned, watching the mansion disappear behind the trees. Someone in Wildewood was growing Wolfsbane for a very specific purpose: to subdue, seduce, and kill the wolves of Wildewood.

But who?

Vargas wasn't acting on his own. He was following someone's directions. Someone else was pulling his strings, just as he had pulled Sophia's.

The truck turned into the safety of our driveway; the engine purred for a moment before Ethan turned it off. Maisie jumped out of the truck, disappearing into the kitchen.

"Do you know what's going on?" I turned toward Ethan.

"I wish I did." He reached for my hand, giving it a squeeze before he climbed out of the truck.

Harold blinked at me, tears still in the corners of his eyes. I patted his head and climbed out of the truck. Snow began to fall, adding an extra chill in the air. I rushed to catch up to Ethan.

I set Harold on the kitchen table and offered him a

kitchen towel to use as a blanket. He wrapped it around his shoulders like a cape. Maisie started making coffee, probably to keep herself busy. Climbing the steps, I changed into a black, crew-neck shirt. Once I was back in the kitchen, I plopped into a chair and watched Harold snuggle the towel against his shoulder. The exhaustion of staying up all night was beginning to sink in. I wasn't ready to allow the emotional exhaustion to take hold yet, but I could feel it creeping around the edges.

"Harold, if you know who is growing those plants, please tell me. They're dangerous."

Maisie placed a cup of coffee in front of me. I wrapped my hands around it. She put a small bowl of cream in front of Harold and he licked his lips.

"Harold." Agatha appeared behind me.

He jumped and spilled the cream across the table.

I glared at her. "Stop scaring him!" I stood, grabbing another kitchen towel that hung on the oven door to clean up the spill.

Agatha rolled her eyes, exhaling sharply through her nose. "I didn't mean to scare you."

My attention returned to the little hobgoblin. "You were about to tell me who is growing those plants . . ."

Harold took in a shaky breath, his little chest swelling. He exhaled hard enough for me to feel his breath against my skin. "Angela."

The cream-soaked towel fell to the floor. My knees gave out and I hit the back of the chair, the front legs lifting off the floor as I fell into it. I looked at Maisie. Her eyes were large, her lips parted, and her brows scrunched. She looked at me and shook her head. How could that be? How could our mother be taking care of a greenhouse?

"Impossible." Agatha moved closer, pointing her index finger at the frightened hobgoblin. "Don't lie to us, you little bat."

"Harold can't lie." He picked up the empty dish and held it in front of him. "You know Harold can't lie!"

I stood so abruptly that the chair fell backward and hit the ground. I ran to the front door, grabbing my bag and pulled out the gift tag from the present that had been left at the café with the skeleton key. Rushing back into the kitchen, I forced my voice to stay calm, "Maisie, get your journal."

Before Maisie and I met, she had received a letter telling her to go to Wildewood. It hadn't been signed or stamped. One sentence had been written in a flowy script: *In Wildewood, you will find your sister, Riley Jones.* I had always assumed Agatha had sent it.

Adrenaline pumped through my veins. I placed the tag on the counter and balled my shaking hands into fists, taking deep breaths to keep myself calm. But it was useless. Maisie walked from her room with the leather-bound journal in her hands. She unwrapped the string that kept it closed, and pulled out the folded note. She placed it beside the gift tag.

The handwriting matched.

"Could our mother . . ." I looked at Agatha. She looked as shocked as I felt. My voice shook, "Could our mother be alive?"

I only ever wanted two things in my life: to know the parents who abandoned me and to be happy. Those things had a tendency to conflict with one another, but with the idea that my mother might still be alive, they went to war.

It felt as if my heart had been ripped out of my chest and shattered into a million pieces as I watched Agatha grasping for words. For once, she was speechless. There was no snarky comment to share. Her eyes locked with mine and she shook her head in disbelief.

Hurt barely described the way I felt. Heartbroken and confused only scratched the surface. My limbs felt like noodles as I picked the chair back up and plopped onto it. Resting my forehead on the table, I took a deep breath. Maisie sat beside me, her hand found mine and I rolled my head to the side to look at her.

I just had one question: Who all knew?

Chapter 45

The shower I took after we got back proved Connie's poultice *had* acted like a glue. After vigorous scrubbing, the black substance had finally come off to reveal a completely healed wound. The shower may have helped my body feel better, but it had done nothing for the ache in my heart. I was exhausted, but I couldn't sleep, even with Ethan's arms wrapped around me. There was too much on my mind.

Tiptoeing from the loft, Ethan fast asleep in my bed, I crept down the stairs. Laying my boots on the steps, I gently closed Maisie's door, not wanting to wake her. I took a seat next to my boots on the bottom stair and pulled them on. No one needed to know what I was about to do. I didn't want company and I especially didn't want anyone talking me out of it.

Standing, I walked to the front door and unclipped the lit-tle broom from the keychain. At the rate I was going through brooms, I might need to consider keeping a few extras around. Holding the broom in my palm, it shook as it grew in size. It was still early morning but the rest of Wildewood would already be awake. They did not have the same night we did. I could take

Ethan's truck, but it was loud. It was a risk flying during the day, but I didn't care.

I was going to get some answers from the only person I knew to hold them. Walking to the back door, Agatha materialized in my way. Dammit. I had forgotten about her.

"Where are you going?"

"Town Hall." The mayor would be in by now. Some days I swore she lived there.

"People will see you." Agatha stepped out of my way.

I raised an eyebrow. She was letting me go without an argument? That was unlike her, but I wasn't going to press it on the chance she changed her mind. "I'll be careful."

I opened the door and stepped out into the early morning sun. The snow from the night before was already melting. The sky was clear; no clouds to hide behind. Agatha followed, watching me as I mounted the broom. I looked at her, she seemed to have more to say but drew her lips into a thin line, wrinkles forming around her mouth.

"I didn't know that she might still be alive."

"I believe you." The broom rose into the air, my feet hovering above the porch.

"I would have told you." She rose with me.

"Agatha, I believe you." Was she feeling guilty because of all the secrets she'd kept from us? Good. Maybe she would think twice the next time.

Her hand touched mine, and for a second I thought I could feel warmth. She flickered, patted my hand, then vanished in wispy black smoke.

Here goes nothing. I hunkered down against the broom handle and whispered, "*Subvolare*."

I soared into the air, away from the safety of my porch. Hovering above the tree line, I took a longer route to stay away from the center of Wildewood where I knew I'd be spotted. As much as I claimed I didn't care, I did. It scared me.

In a matter of minutes, my feet touched the back steps of Town Hall. I tried the doorknob, and when it wouldn't budge, I whispered, "*Reserare*." The lock clicked, the knob turned.

I stepped into the hallway, catching Esther walking into her office. She backed out of it, her head cocked and a single brow raised, seeing me with the broom by my side as if it were a staff.

"I need to speak with you."

"Come on," she walked back into her office.

I leaned the broom beside the back door, relieved she hadn't scolded me or put up her usual "I'm busy" argument. I chased after her before she could change her mind and sat in the chair across from her desk.

"I figured this conversation was due." She sat in her thick, leather rolling chair.

Okay, good. Did this mean she wasn't going to hide things from me any longer? That would be a nice change, but we'd see how long it would last.

"I want to know about my mother." My fingers dug into the armrest.

"Anything specific?" She leaned back in her chair, crossing her legs at the knees.

"Well, for starters . . . is she alive?" My chest tightened as I waited for her response. I didn't know which answer I wanted to hear. If she was alive, would I finally meet the mother who abandoned me almost three decades ago? If the answer was no, then I'd never have the chance.

"Yes."

Licking my lips, tears stung my eyes. I wiped them away before they could fall and took in a deep breath. Having difficulty swallowing, I croaked out, "Where is she?"

"Twin Falls."

Of course, because Twin Falls had everything we didn't—including my mother. "Where in Twin Falls?"

Esther readjusted her legs, recrossing the other leg on top. "There is a place tucked away in the mountain. Before you ask, it has no official name. No one knows of its existence unless you need to know about it and most people do not need to know."

"Why is she there?"

Esther pursed her lips. Her eyes met mine. "She was a danger to Wildewood. After your birth"—she stopped and moved the chair closer to the desk to lean on her arms—"Agatha came to me and begged me to lock her away before she hurt you or Maisie."

Hurt us? Wait—I closed my eyes—did this mean my mother hadn't abandoned us but instead was forced to give us up? My chest tightened. If she hadn't been locked away in this 'hole' in Twin Falls, would she have kept us? Raised us? Together?

Taking a shaky breath, I pushed the hurt that was forming down as deep as I could. I still had more questions that needed answers. I couldn't get off track, though what I really wanted to do was scream at Esther, at Agatha, and anyone else who'd played a part in our separation.

"After she . . . *left* . . . how did the wolf pack acquire Peaceful Acres?" I assumed, since the mansion was on the land, it might have once belonged to the Wildewoods too. "And why?"

"After your mother went away, the alpha was charged with keeping the mansion secure."

"Why does it need to be secure?" It's only a house, right? A large, possibly haunted, house. Though, now that Agatha lived with me, maybe it wasn't haunted anymore. Unless I had more dead aunts than just her.

"*It* doesn't, but the contents inside could cause havoc if removed. There is a lot about your family you still don't know."

I didn't know anything about my family, because everyone in this damn town kept it a secret. It's as if we were the town pariahs. Don't talk about it and maybe it'll go away. Well, it wasn't going away. *We* weren't going away.

"Okay . . ." I ran a hand over my face. "The alpha is in charge of keeping the contents of the mansion inside the mansion. Is it safe to assume that Vargas knows about something he wants to get his hands on, and that's why he wanted control?"

"I would say that's a safe assumption, but who knows."

"Why couldn't you just lock it up?" She was a powerful witch, couldn't she place a spell over the mansion to keep it locked? Someone had already hidden the entrance, so why not go one step further?

"I did." She narrowed her eyes at me. I watched her eyes soften then grow large as if she had thought of something. Esther stood, her chair hitting the bookcase behind it. She moved around her desk to the door and peeked out then glanced over her shoulder. "Come with me."

I followed her to the vault. She opened it with a wave of her hand before we hit the bottom step. Rushing inside, she bent down to a locked drawer of a tall, wooden cabinet. Rummaging around, papers slipped out and floated to the floor, items clinked together. Her fingers gripped the edge of the drawer and she let out a loud sigh then slammed it shut. "It's gone."

"What's gone?"

She moved to a large, wooden trunk further in the room. After a few moments of digging through it, she slammed the lid with a frustrated cry, causing me to jump. This was out of character; Esther was usually poised and calm.

"Esther, what is missing?"

She straightened her posture, smoothing out her coat by pulling on the ends. Turning, she looked at me. "The key."

I walked to a small trunk nestled beside the larger one and pushed it open. "What does it look like? Maybe I can help find it."

"It's not here." She pushed on the lid of the trunk my hands were in.

I yelped, moving them out of the way before they were crushed. "Can you at least tell me what the key is for? Is it to unlock the mansion?"

I followed her back up the stairs. The vault door slammed shut behind us, the click and spin of the handle echoed through the space.

"It's not *just* a key, Riley." She marched into her office. "I set up an elaborate spell to lock the mansion. I should've known something was wrong when that little creature—your shadow—appeared." Esther plopped into her desk chair. She tapped her finger to her chin, her brows drawn down. "Our *beloved* sheriff must've gotten his hands on it. I just don't know how."

Dread washed over me. Could Harold have given Vargas the key? Did he take it when he found the grimoire or the pendulum? I chewed on the inside of my cheek. Oh, Harold. What did you do?

"Riley, there is something you need to know about the key." Esther leaned forward, her elbows resting on her desk. "Something I thought only two people knew—myself and Eugene."

"What?" I lowered into the chair opposite her.

"For it to work, to remove my spell, it requires the willing blood of a wolf *and* a witch. Specifically, the blood has to come from the alpha and either a Wildewood or a Keeper."

I swallowed, staring at my hands in my lap. "That's why Vargas—"

"Wanted to become alpha, yes. I think so."

I looked up at her, the dread gripping me tighter. Esther's chest rose and fell as she took in a deep breath. "Who would be helping him?"

"I think the question is, who would need his help?"

I didn't know what else to say. I gathered my broom, deciding to walk back home. How was I supposed to break this news to Maisie? Harold had already told us our mother was maintaining the greenhouse, but how was that possible if she was locked away? Rubbing my temple, a headache forming, I just didn't understand. She had gotten to Vargas, so maybe she had someone else, on her behalf, growing the Wolfsbane?

Nothing made sense to me anymore.

I walked inside the little cottage, hanging my jacket on the coat rack. I slid my boots off, my toes relieved to be out of their confines then padded through the house to Maisie's door. I pushed it open. She was still asleep, her breathing soft. I hated to wake her up, but she needed to know everything the mayor had divulged. This was not something I felt I could keep from her.

Sitting on the edge of her bed, I nudged her shoulder. She blinked groggily, looking at me, and rubbed the sleep from her eyes. "What's wrong?" She sat up against the headboard.

I took a deep breath. "She's alive."

The corners of her mouth turned down. "Are you sure?"

No, not really. I wouldn't believe it until I saw her with my own eyes. I shook my head and shrugged. "I'm going to find out."

Chapter 46

Maisie decided to go back to work for the evening shift, even after I assured her it would be okay for the café to stay closed one more day but she insisted and I didn't argue. I had a feeling she needed something to help take her mind off the events that had transpired in the last twenty-four hours. But I had something I needed to do. One last thing before I could move on from the events of last week and digest the information I had learned if that were even possible.

The automatic doors of the hospital swooshed open and I walked into the sterile waiting room. It was mostly empty, besides a mother and her little boy sitting against the far wall. I spotted the nurse who had helped me when the wolf had attacked. Ashley, I think her name was. Thank goodness I already knew the room Eugene was in, so I slinked away, hoping and praying she wouldn't see me.

The only problem—I was carrying a bright yellow "Get Well Soon" balloon. She turned her head, squinting as if trying to place me. I quickened my pace toward the double doors that led into the hallway where the patient rooms were.

"Hey, Miss!" she called after me but the doors had shut and, whoops, I couldn't hear her.

Finding the room Eugene was in, I pushed the balloon through the door. Juggling the half-dozen muffins in my arms, I could still feel the warmth they generated through the bottom of the box. Moving the balloon out of my way, I stilled at the sight of Eugene. He was bruised and broken. His foot was held up in a sling and his leg wrapped in a white bandage. His skin was splotched in deep-purple bruises and his right eye was swollen shut.

Ethan told me werewolves healed quickly, but he had not improved much since the night at Peaceful Acres. Perhaps his body had to deal with the internal effects of the poison before it could heal the other injuries. But he was alive. His body would heal, eventually.

Eugene looked away from Michael, sitting next to the bed in a light-blue chair. A big grin spread across his face. "There you are!" He motioned for me to come closer.

Officer Russell stood on the other side in plain clothes. I couldn't keep the surprise off my face, having never seen him in anything but his uniform. He tipped his head in my direction. He and Michael moved away from the bed to give me some room. Russell clapped his hand on Michael's shoulder. "Let's give them a moment. I'll buy you a coffee."

Coffee? I raised a brow at Russell. Wow, another surprise. The corners of his lips twitched, and he pulled an unopened tea bag from his pocket. I should've known better. Michael mouthed a "thank you." He wrapped his arms around my shoulders in a tight hug before leaving with Russell.

Setting the muffins on the tray near Eugene's bed, I let go of the balloon. The weight attached to the string drifted to the floor. Eugene reached his hand out, and I placed my smaller one in his.

"I owe you." He patted my hand gently.

Tears clouded my vision, and I choked back a laugh. "I'm just glad you're alive."

Eugene grunted. "Whatever was in that nasty drink,"—he shrugged—"well, it brought me back." He kissed the top of my hand before letting it go to reach for the box of muffins. "Michael said you were working on a spell to help find me."

Wolves could smell a witch, I had to remind myself. Even with this knowledge, it felt strange to be open about what I was and what I could do. I gave Eugene a weak smile. "He never stopped looking for you."

"Michael is a good kid." Eugene took a bite from the top of a lemon-blueberry muffin. I didn't know what his favorite muffin was, so there were six different flavors.

I took the seat Michael had been in, and I watched him for a moment. He closed his eyes as he took another bite, mumbling something about the horrible cafeteria food. He peeked at me. "What's on your mind?"

"Can I ask you a question?"

"Of course." He pulled the rest of the paper from the bottom of the muffin and laid it on the tray.

"When you were at The Witches Brew working on the ovens"—the chair squeaked as I leaned forward—"I overheard you telling Michael things had changed."

Eugene stopped eating. He swallowed and set the muffin down.

"What did you mean?" I watched him closely as he dusted crumbs from his blanket.

He straightened up as much as his broken leg would allow. "You weren't supposed to hear that," he muttered under his breath.

Sighing, I placed my hand on the bed and looked into his eyes. "What has changed? Were you talking about Vargas?"

Eugene licked his lips and he shook his head. I noticed the numbers on the machine monitoring his blood pressure were rising. "Vargas was only a pawn."

I had figured as much. "Who was manipulating him?"

Eugene glanced around the room. He licked his lips. I had never seen Eugene squirm before.

"Please tell me. I can't deal with any more secrets."

His eyes finally landed on me. He took in a deep breath. "For twenty-eight years, this town managed to keep what we are a secret from the outside world. We had no issues, no serious crime. Wildewood was a safe town for . . . non-humans. We kept to ourselves, and only ever went to Twin Falls for things that couldn't be found here," Eugene paused, his lips thinned and he looked at me. "We always knew one day the Wildewoods would return."

There it was. "And now? Now that we're back?" What shift could our return have caused?

"You girls weren't what we were worried about."

My stomach dropped. "Who then?"

Eugene exhaled and leaned his head back, staring at the ceiling. His silence, though only a few seconds, became maddening.

"Dammit, Eugene!" I pounded my fist on the bed, my patience depleted. "Is my mom back in town?" Could she have been released or have escaped?

Eugene swallowed audibly. "I'm not sure."

I buried my head in my hands and let out a frustrated cry.

"Esther told me she was locked away in Twin Falls, the same place Vargas went to. Do you know if she's still there?"

He licked his lips, nodding. "I paid her a visit after Sasha passed."

The door to the room opened before I had a chance to digest what he said. Michael stepped inside and glanced between the two of us, worry nestling between his brows in a deep crease. I stood, deciding it was time for me to leave before I fell apart. I gave Michael a small smile, though it took every ounce of effort. I wrapped my arms around my torso, glancing back at Eugene.

"Will you take me to see her?" If he wouldn't, I'd find out myself where exactly this place was. But it would be a lot easier with some help.

"Riley, no." Eugene shook his head.

"You said you owe me." I licked my suddenly dry lips and hugged myself tighter, trying to suppress the shaking of my shoulders. "I'll give you time to heal, but you will take me to her." I walked out of the room, my pace quickening down the hallway the further I got. Right before the double doors, John Russell stood beside a trash can, throwing his tea bag into it.

"Riley?" He glanced up at me, but I kept walking, afraid to answer in case the almost thirty years of pain were to rush out.

I could no longer contain the shaking of my shoulders, my vision blurred with tears that traveled down my cheeks, wetting my jacket. I didn't even bother to wipe them away. What was the point? The dam had broken. I hiked back to town, not wanting to use the cab service available at the hospital. Maybe by the time I got to the café, to Maisie, I would regain my composure.

But as I walked into the café, and Maisie looked up at me from behind the register, all the hurt came out in a cry and I shattered, falling to my knees. Maisie ran to me and put her hands on either side of my face, raising it so I had to look at her.

"Is she . . ." her voice failed as a single tear ran down her cheek.

I swallowed, nodding my head.

Our mother was alive.

To be continued . . .

Acknowledgements

Big shout out to my friends and family for supporting me through the various stages of book two.

To my husband, thank you for being brave enough to tell me the issues you found in the first draft. I think I handled it 'relatively' well . . . Without you, chasing my dreams would be even more difficult. I love you to the Pegasus galaxy and back!

To Terri, thank you for being a speed reader and helping me as much as you have!

To my betas, you guys rock! I am so appreciative of the time you took out of your days to read A Deadly Secret. Thank you from the bottom of my heart!

To my children (especially the little ones), because of all four of you, I've learned to tune out A LOT of noise and write during chaos.

About the Author

R.M. Connor lives in Georgia with her handsome hubby and their four children. She has been a writer since her early teens and has always dreamed of becoming a published author. She spends her days chasing small children and daydreaming about her books. She loves metal, rock music, carnivorous plants and is a huge Trekkie.

Follow her to stay up to date for the next book of
The Deadly Series

Instagram: @R.M.Connor_writes

Facebook: R.M. Connor

Website: www.rmconnor.com